"G

Linda slowly obeyed.

Tate brought her palm up to his chest where he gently spread her fingers against his warmth. His voice was edged with huskiness as he said, "I know we haven't had a lot of time. So many things have been happening, but... Do you feel that?"

Linda's eyes were huge as she looked up at him. His heart was beating strongly beneath her hand. Vibrant, alive. She felt herself begin to tremble.

"It's yours," he said simply.

Linda caught her breath. So many things *had* happened. She wasn't sure she was still the same person she used to be. But she was certain of two things: her abiding love for her sister, and her newly found love for this man.

"I love you, Linda," Tate said softly. "I want you to be my wife."

ABOUT THE AUTHOR

Ginger Chambers gets story ideas from a variety of sources. Sometimes she starts with a specific character in mind, puts the person in a situation and watches as the action starts to evolve. In *Passages of Gold* she took her research one step farther and actually went panning. A native of Texas, Ginger makes her home in northern California with her husband and two teenagers.

Books by Ginger Chambers

HARLEQUIN AMERICAN ROMANCE

32–GAME OF HEARTS
71–PASSION'S PREY
107–IN LOVE'S SHADOW
169–WHEN HEARTS COLLIDE
238–FIREFLY IN THE NIGHT
254–CALL MY NAME SOFTLY

Don't miss any of our special offers. Write to us at the following address for information on our newest releases.

Harlequin Reader Service
901 Fuhrmann Blvd., P.O. Box 1397, Buffalo, NY 14240
Canadian address: P.O. Box 603,
Fort Erie, Ont. L2A 5X3

Passages of Gold
Ginger Chambers

Harlequin Books

TORONTO • NEW YORK • LONDON
AMSTERDAM • PARIS • SYDNEY • HAMBURG
STOCKHOLM • ATHENS • TOKYO • MILAN

This book is for my family—
aunts, uncles and cousins—
who saw my mother through her illness
when I was far away.

And to my mother, Annie,
who proves that gold is not merely
a precious metal.

Published March 1989

First printing January 1989

ISBN 0-373-16288-X

Copyright © 1989 by Ginger Chambers. All rights reserved.
Except for use in any review, the reproduction or utilization
of this work in whole or in part in any form by any electronic,
mechanical or other means, now known or hereafter invented,
including xerography, photocopying and recording,
or in any information storage or retrieval system, is forbidden without
the permission of the publisher, Harlequin Enterprises Limited,
225 Duncan Mill Road, Don Mills, Ontario, Canada M3B 3K9.

All the characters in this book have no existence outside the
imagination of the author and have no relation whatsoever to
anyone bearing the same name or names. They are not even
distantly inspired by any individual known or unknown to the
author, and all incidents are pure invention.

® are Trademarks registered in the United States Patent and
Trademark Office and in other countries.

Printed in U.S.A.

Chapter One

Tate Winslow sat in his crowded office, trying to ignore the clamor that was taking place in the hallway outside. In his hand was a letter. In his eyes were the shadows of memories both good and bad...but mostly bad.

"Please! You *have* to help me...." The voice rushed into the room like a sudden windstorm, disturbing the leaves of memory, causing them to dance in tiny whirlwinds before being swept away.

Tate looked up, focused his eyes and saw the cause of the disturbance. One of his students—one who had played around for most of the semester, gracing the lecture room with sporadic visits and rarely doing his work—was now facing him with panic etched on his face. Under other circumstances, Tate would have made a wry remark that held a stinging edge. But at this moment, for his own reasons, he was glad to be dragged back to the present.

"What can I do to help you, Martin?" he asked. The weariness of his voice was not calculated. He could banish the memories, but not their effect on him.

The student rushed into an explanation Tate had heard many times before: he now saw the error of his ways, he hadn't realized his grade was so perilously perched, he had been sick a lot, he had been needed at home.... He threw in everything but a fatal disease.

Tate was still as Martin Klousky went through his spiel and remained still even as he finished. Then he moved, shifting position in his chair. "What course do I teach, Martin?"

The young man was quick with an answer. "History. In my case, History 141."

"The Study of the Growth of Western Culture," Tate mused, fixing his dark brown gaze on his student. "Have you read the book?"

"What book, sir?" Martin Klousky sensed trouble.

"Your textbook. The one you were supposed to buy at the beginning of the semester. You did buy it....?"

"Of course. Yes, sir."

"And in your reading, what did you learn?"

"That history has a way of repeating itself?"

Tate smiled. He knew Martin was bluffing. With more than a touch of sarcasm he said, "Very good! Now... if you want a passing grade from me, you're going to have to work for it. I want an analysis of at least six instances when history did seem to repeat itself, with emphasis on the political and economic aspects. Because you see, Martin, I want *you* to learn something from this. It's easier to come to class and to do the work like all the other poor slogs than it is to race in at the end of the semester and throw yourself on the mercy of the lecturer. Some professors don't have much mercy... unlike me."

"You call this mercy?" Martin's face was stricken.

"I call it fair play."

Martin grumbled something beneath his breath as he turned to leave the room.

"What was that?" Tate asked, pretending curiosity.

The young man swiveled a resentful face back toward him, but quickly smothered his feelings. "I said I'll get it to you."

"By the date of the final—oh, and you *will* have to take the final. I think that would only be fair, too, don't you?"

"Fair to who?" Martin challenged him.

"To yourself," Tate replied, the words quiet.

Martin gazed at him silently before finally exiting the room.

When he was once again alone, Tate sighed. He could hear the words "It's not fair!" echoing through the corridors of time, coming in his own angry young voice, directed at the man whose letter he now held.

"Nobody ever said anything in this world was fair, son."

Son. He had called him son. But he was no relation.

A timid tapping sounded on the door, before another student opened it far enough to peek inside.

"Give me a few minutes, Rebecca, please. I—" The head instantly disappeared. How many more were out there? he wondered. This had been going on for days. Had his program been exceptionally complicated this year? Or had circumstances gathered to make this semester particularly difficult for everyone?

He liked teaching at Montclair College. It was small, barely eight hundred students. It was private. He also liked the location, tucked into a quiet valley in far Northern California. And the pay was pretty good.

He had found a niche for himself. A niche he didn't want to be prodded from, which was exactly what would happen if he did what the letter asked.

Again he saw himself as a child. Hostile to the world, burdened with a father who regularly disgraced himself and who didn't seem to care what became of his only son—whether he had clothing, clean or unclean, food for that night or the next morning.

Patrick McHenry had helped him then. He had seen the emotional and physical abuse the eleven-year-old had been suffering and had stepped in to lighten it.

If it hadn't been for Patrick...

Tate looked about the room, letting his eyes follow the lines of books on the narrow shelves, letting them dwell on the stacks of papers that spilled from his desk onto the floor—term papers from each of his classes that were in various stages of being graded.

If he had continued the way he was going—alienated from his father, alienated from everyone else in the world—he probably would have ended up in jail. Patrick's action had changed his life, and he owed almost everything he had achieved since to him...yet he wished he hadn't received this letter.

Over the years he and his old mentor had exchanged periodic messages, telling each other how life was now treating them. Telling about their plans, their dreams—the dreams were mostly his, not Patrick's. Patrick was content with his life in the tiny gold mining community where he had been the sheriff for the past forty-two years. Just as Tate had carved a place for himself at Montclair College, Patrick had done the same in Amador Springs.

Amador Springs... Even thinking the name caused a shiver of distaste to run up Tate's spine. He had escaped from the place, turned his back on his past, made a new life. He didn't think of it often, only when he addressed a letter to Patrick, and then he put it out of his mind as quickly as was humanly possible.

And now this.

He brought the letter into view again. The words hadn't changed. He couldn't rearrange them. He couldn't will them away. Patrick needed his help. It was the only time the man had ever asked him for anything.

Tate ran a long-fingered hand through his dark hair as panic coursed through him. When his hand came back to rest on the chair arm, he could see that it was trembling.

He had an excuse. He and Miriam were going to take a tour through Greece. Her specialty was philosophy, his was classical history. What better place to go? They had been planning the trip for the past two summers, but something had always seemed to get in the way, just as something always seemed to stop him from deepening his commitment to her. He told himself that it was her, that she was too independent to want him as anything more than an occasional lover. Their relationship was comfortable, nonbinding, very adult. How would Miriam take this newest setback to their plans if he decided to go back to Amador Springs?

If he decided to go back?

The tapping on his door sounded once more. Tate shut the letter away in his top desk drawer and called for the student to enter. This time the problem wasn't a passing grade but the need for an A+ rather than an A−. What could she do to bring up her grade?

Tate listened to Rebecca's words of woe with only partial attention. Most of his thoughts were centered on his desk, on the letter pleading for his help—not in actual words, Patrick was too proud for that, but very evident in the tone.

Could he come to any other decision than yes?

Chapter Two

"I just don't know. I can't tell—" The rustle of paper accompanied the muted words as Linda Conway turned the map this way and that, while also trying to consult directions written on a separate scrap of paper. "The road should be coming up, but—" More rattling of paper, more consternation that was quickly growing into an almost hysterical need to succeed in finding her way.

Taking a deep breath, she tried to calm herself. It wasn't as if she were traversing the outback of Australia or going upriver along the Amazon. She was in California, for heaven's sake! Civilization wasn't that far away. Only at the moment did it seem as if it were. She had been driving for so long along narrow twisting roads, getting farther and farther into the rugged terrain of what was supposed to be gold rush country. And she was getting more and more lost.

The directions she had with her did little good. They didn't correspond to the map. Where one intersecting road was supposed to be, it wasn't; and where another wasn't supposed to be, it was.

Linda let her hands fall, crushing the map beneath them. What she had once looked upon as salvation was fast becoming nothing less than another living hell.

She glanced at her sister asleep on the back seat, her frail body curled in exhaustion, her blond hair, so like her own, framing a face that looked haunted even in repose. Guilt immediately flashed through her, causing her to turn back around. Melanie was relying on her; she had always relied upon her.

Linda lifted the map again and consulted the written directions with a fierceness that dared them to be mistaken. She *would* find the gold claim. There *would* be gold there. Then all their problems would be solved.

As she continued to study the papers, a haze of moisture blurred her vision and it wasn't until she blinked the film away that sense slowly began to emerge from the puzzle. She wasn't as lost as she had thought. She had only been confused, had mistaken one turn for another and given up too soon.

Restarting the car, she pulled back onto the roadway.

A SHORT TIME LATER they arrived at their destination—or at least what Linda thought was their destination. She reached into the back seat and nudged Melanie awake.

"What— What is it? Are we there?" her sister asked as she groggily pushed herself upright.

"As far as I can tell," Linda replied tersely.

Melanie blinked at the brightness of the midmorning sun, brushing the fine hair away from her face, where it had settled during her sleep. "Are you sure?" she asked, examining their unpromising surroundings.

"Not really." Linda thrust open her door and stepped outside. Melanie soon followed suit and the two sisters stood in momentary silence. Then Linda pointed. "It should be right down there."

Rocks and brush and a variety of spindly trees hid the stream from view, but the gurgle of water could be heard as it burbled its way from one point to another downstream.

"Linda, I'm not so sure about this," Melanie said softly.

"It'll be all right," Linda answered, steeling her heart to the fear she heard behind her sister's words. They had to do this; they had no other choice. "Come on."

She set off along a path of sorts, pushing against the trailers of brush that tugged at her denim-covered legs. She heard Melanie follow her after only a slight hesitation.

It was with great relief that a few moments later Linda discovered the marker that the directions said would signal their late uncle's claim: a large oak tree with a split trunk and a great black gnarl growing several feet above ground at the fork. It was positioned along the ridge of an embankment that lined a miniature canyon. On the far side, a sheer cliff jutted into the sky. In the middle was the stream. This was it. They had arrived. She hadn't been sure until...

Next to her she felt Melanie stiffen. She glanced at her sister in surprised curiosity before thinking to search for the cause.

The stream was fairly narrow at this point, bedded in rock, with a wide expanse of sun-bleached boulders and gravel on either side. A short distance downstream it curved out of view. However Linda's gaze didn't attempt to probe the distance. Her attention immediately centered on the man who was kneeling at the edge of the stream, washing something in the water. Then it moved to the other man, who was forced to duck his head as he came out of a wooden lean-to.

They were both big men, tall and brawny; one with a woolly black beard, the other without. Both were wearing work-worn clothing. The bearded man stood up, and Linda could see that he was holding a couple of plates and a pot that he had been washing in the stream.

"Who—?" Melanie started to ask.

"I don't know," Linda hastily replied in a whisper.

Both women immediately faded behind the tree. Masculine laughter was carried on the breeze along with words that neither Linda nor Melanie understood.

"You said you weren't sure—" Melanie started again.

"This tree says we're right. It's described exactly." She thrust the paper toward her sister.

"I believe you," Melanie assured her without taking it. Her eyes returned to the men as she peeked carefully around the trunk. "So who are they?"

"I guess we'll have to find that out."

"How?"

"Ask them."

"But they look—"

"Rough, I know."

Passages of Gold

"Maybe there's been some kind of mistake. Maybe Uncle Roger didn't own the claim. Maybe he only thought he did. Maybe he gave—"

"Shh! One of them is looking this way."

They adjusted their positions behind the tree, not yet ready to be seen. Several long seconds passed, seconds in which Linda thought they would be the ones challenged. But the men started talking again. Once more there was a bark of laughter.

"I want to go home, Linda. I don't think I like it here."

Linda raked a hand through her hair. They couldn't go home. Not now. Not for a long time. She said, "Be quiet. Let me think." And immediately softened the edge from her words when she felt her sister wither. "There probably is some kind of mistake, but it's them who's made it. This *is* Uncle's claim. I'm sure of it."

She took a deep breath and stepped away from the cover of the tree. "Stay here," she hissed at her sister, hoping that she would obey.

Linda took several steps before the bearded man looked up. She saw his body stiffen and his partner immediately copied his action. She smiled, continuing to move closer, yet careful to keep the water separating them.

"Good afternoon," she called.

Neither man replied.

She tried again. "I was wondering if you could help me."

Still neither man replied, neither man moved. Their eyes were fixed on her as if she were an apparition.

She stopped at the water's edge. "I'm trying to find the claim of Roger Conway. I know it's around here somewhere and I wondered if you might be able to help me."

Finally the clean-shaven man moved, relaxing his stance. "Never heard of him," he said.

"But he lived around here for twenty years. Surely..."

"I still never heard of him," the man repeated.

Linda slipped her fingers into the back pockets of her jeans and thumped a rock with the toe of one boot. "I have directions...they brought me here."

"Your directions are wrong," the other man growled, only to be hushed by a quick cautionary movement of his partner's hand.

The partner smiled, softening his expression. "There has to be some kind of mistake. We've been working this claim for two years. It's ours. Is it possible your directions are wrong?"

"It's possible," Linda admitted. She was becoming less sure of herself by the second. "But that tree..." she said, turning slightly, motioning toward the split tree trunk.

The friendlier man laughed. "There are trees like that all over the place. Bugs get in 'em when they're young. You better keep looking. This isn't the right place."

Linda frowned. "And you didn't know my uncle?"

"No, ma'am."

Linda shrugged. "Well...I'm sorry I disturbed you." She hesitated. "Ah...is there anyone else around here who might know—?"

She was interrupted. "I'm sorry, ma'am. I guess my partner and I don't make friends easily. We kinda stick to ourselves."

Linda climbed back up the incline toward the tree. As she gained higher ground, she glanced back, only to see that the man holding the dishes was still watching her.

"What are we going to do?" Melanie asked as they returned to the car.

Linda reached for the map and consulted it again. "A town's not too far away. Let's go there and ask. Surely someone will remember Uncle Roger. I know he was a bit reclusive—but a person can't live twenty years in an area without someone remembering him. He had to go in for supplies."

"He was crazy as a coot. That's what Daddy always said."

"Daddy thought anybody who didn't like ranching was crazy."

"Yes, but..."

"If Uncle Roger hadn't come here, he wouldn't have left us the claim. And if he hadn't left us the claim..."

Melanie bit her bottom lip. As she slid into the front passenger seat, she murmured, "We're probably crazy as coots, too."

For the first time in a long while Linda gave a genuine smile. It had also been a long time since Melanie attempted even so mild a joke. The trip to California already was doing them good, even if they hadn't yet accomplished any of their goals.

THE TOWN of Amador Springs was so small it was barely there. It had the look of a once-thriving community, but now all that was left were memories. It was too far off the tourist track to draw visitors, and the people who remained must have liked it that way. The town boasted two service stations, one of which was so dilapidated looking that it must have been closed for some time. It was to the remaining station, also fairly run-down, that Linda maneuvered the car.

A man shuffled out of a small building, where age had taken its toll, just as it had on him.

"Fill'er up?" he questioned.

Linda nodded, and as he fumbled with the gas cap and nozzle, she got out of the car and walked to where he was standing.

"Right pretty day," he observed.

"Sure is," she replied.

"You two just passing through?" he asked.

Linda knew his kind—one of the town gossips. If she was going to get information, she would surely get it from him.

"Actually, no. My sister and I are here to see about our uncle's claim. He left it to us in his will. His name was Roger Conway. Did you know him?"

"Roger?" the old man repeated, his gaze turning to examine her more closely. "You're kin to Roger?"

Linda nodded. "You knew him?"

"'Course I knew him. Too bad about what happened to him. But I guess accidents do happen. Happen all the time. Only..." He stopped, turning his keen gaze back to the job at hand.

"Only what?" she prompted.

"Nothin'." His response was clipped. He finished topping off the tank and moved to clean the windows. "Want me to check your oil?"

"I'd appreciate it." Linda released the hood latch from inside the car, then went to stand beside him again. "As I said, my sister and I have come to take over his claim...only we can't seem to find it. Do you know where it's located?"

"Sure I do. Oil's okay." He slammed down the hood.

Linda dug into her pocket for some money. She handed it to him. "I have some instructions. Do you think you could look at them and tell me if they're right?"

"Give 'em to me."

Linda reached into Melanie's open window for the scrap of paper.

The man took it in his arthritic hands and studied the wording for a moment. He handed it back. "That's the place, all right. Go back upstream a few miles, go over a couple of hills, then over a narrow bridge...and take the first turn to your right after the bridge."

Linda frowned. That sounded close to what they had already done. But possibly *close* wasn't good enough. "Thanks," she said, settling back into the car.

The old man ambled toward the window, not yet through with the conversation. "So you two are goin' to work Roger's claim?"

"We sure are."

"Heard a rumor that there's more gold comin' down."

"I wouldn't know," Linda replied.

The keen old eyes became amused. "Well, good luck anyway," he called and stepped back when Linda started the engine.

As they pulled out of the station, Melanie chided, "Why did you say that? We *know* there's gold—at least that there's some, because that's what the lawyer said."

"But we don't want to put it around, do we?"

"No, I guess not."

"Not that he was fooled."

"He?"

"The old man. Didn't you see the way he smiled? But a person can't just admit— Anyway, we don't know how much there is. And we still have the small problem of finding it."

"The claim?"

"Actually I was thinking of the gold. It doesn't just jump out of the ground, you know."

When Melanie lapsed into silence at the tartness of her tone, Linda wished that she had kept her momentary pessimism to herself.

THE OLD MAN'S directions led them to backtrack all the way to the secluded clearing where they had parked their car once before.

"So this *was* the place," Melanie breathed.

"Looks like it." Linda's lips were tight.

"But what about those men?"

Linda didn't answer as she set off through the brush.

They were almost to the tree when Melanie whispered, "I'm not going to hide this time. If we face them, we face them together."

Again Linda didn't answer. She appreciated the spirit behind her sister's determination, but she knew that because of her recent difficulties Melanie would be of little help if the men proved to be a problem. But she didn't say anything to decline the offer. Her younger sister needed every possible morale boost.

The men were still there.

Beside her, Linda heard Melanie's tiny gasp of dismay. It was enough to alert the men to their intrusion. The man without a beard looked up, saw them, and quickly alerted his partner. That man drew a gun from within his shirt as he turned to face them.

At sight of the weapon, Linda's heart froze along with the rest of her body. She didn't know what to do—whether to run, stay still, or drop to the ground as savvy people did in the movies.

"So you're back," the bearded man growled. "And this time you've brought a friend."

Linda didn't like the way he said those words. Suddenly she realized they were in more than one kind of danger and cursed herself for her stupidity. One problem at a time was all her brain seemed able to handle. Her mind had been so full of all the difficulties they had been through recently, and of what could be the solution to most of those problems. She hadn't thought—

"Yes, we're back," she retorted. "And the police aren't far behind us."

"That's nice." The man wasn't impressed.

"This *is* our claim."

"Is that so?"

"Yes."

The man smiled. "You ever hear of squatters' rights?"

Melanie's hand found its way to Linda's arm. She was looking at the men, seemingly fascinated by them. "Let's get out of here, Linda," she whispered. "Nothing's worth—"

The man with the gun waved it slightly. "You think I know how to use this?" he asked.

"Probably." Linda swallowed.

The man took aim and the gravel at their feet puffed into bits of smoke. Both women jumped, startled and shocked.

He took aim again, only this time not at their feet. "We told you once to get out of here," he growled. "We're not going to tell you again. Either you leave, right now, or these next two bullets are going to sting."

Linda heard Melanie's quiet whimper. She reached out to cover her sister's hand and started to back away.

"Get!" the man ordered.

As they plunged into the brush, coarse laughter followed their flight.

BOTH LINDA AND MELANIE were panting as the car careened down the narrow road. Linda hadn't taken the time to turn the vehicle around; they had needed to get out of there right then, without a second of lost time.

The car jerked onto the connecting road, and Linda instinctively turned it toward the little town before taking time to glance at her sister, to see how she was standing up to what had happened. The two of them had been around guns for most of their lives—being

Passages of Gold

raised on a fairly isolated ranch had necessitated that familiarity. But neither had ever had a gun pointed at them...shot at them!

Melanie was pale. She had been ever since the terrible experiences of the past few months. Now she was even paler. Her mouth was thin but it still managed to tremble as she asked, "Do you think they'll follow us?"

"In what? I didn't see a car."

"Neither did I, but that doesn't mean—"

Linda pressed the accelerator to the floor, anger at herself, at the situation, making her reckless. If the little town didn't have a police force, they would go on to the next. They would go all the way to Sacramento if they had to. The events of the past few months had left her feeling almost totally impotent—there had been nothing she could do! She had had her opportunity and blown it. It was because of her that they were in danger of losing the ranch that their family had lived on for generations. Her neglect.

She shook her head, trying to clear it of the thought. Since she seemed to be so single-minded, she couldn't afford to have more than one aim at a time. The past was done, over with. But there was something she could do about the present. The claim was a gift left to them by their uncle. He had worked it under difficult circumstances for far too many years for them to let go of it easily. Anyway, Conways didn't give up, unless the odds were so high that...

She shook her head again and directed another glance at Melanie. Her sister looked so delicate, so fragile, as if a slight breath of wind would tumble her away. Both of them had the same small, thin body type, but she felt so much stronger. She had always felt stronger.

She had to get Melanie settled. If not at the claim, then in the town. Melanie was already worn-out. And now this.

THEY PULLED UP to the same service station that they had visited earlier. The same elderly man shuffled out.

He frowned. "Aren't you the—?"

Linda didn't let him finish. "Do you have a police chief here? A sheriff... a deputy... anyone?"

"Somethin' happen?" the man quizzed, his interest immediately piqued.

Linda dismissed him brusquely. She wasn't in the mood to talk to anyone except a policeman. "Is there one in town? If not, where can I find one?"

The man pointed slowly. "Over there," he said. "Sheriff's office is over there."

Linda's gaze followed the direction he indicated, and she gunned the car out of the station after giving the old man an abrupt word of thanks. As she parked the car she turned to Melanie. "Do you want to wait here?"

"No!" Melanie answered immediately.

Linda opened her door, cursing the fates for what was happening to them. Didn't they deserve an easy time with anything?

Melanie was close behind her as they opened the door and entered the sheriff's office. Inside, the room was tiny, barely able to hold the two desks and small cell it contained. In appearance it was like something out of a cheap movie set. So were the three men, who were in various stages of getting up in reaction to their precipitous arrival.

One was old—the requisite Gabby Hayes character—somewhere in his sixties, with white hair, a bushy white beard and a potbelly that lapped over his low-riding belt.

Another was of medium build and average height, with sandy-blond hair and a matching mustache; he had just the suggestion of a belly.

The third was tall and dark, with dark eyes, strongly crafted cheekbones and a finely drawn nose and mouth. His hair, longer than usual for an officer, curled lightly onto his neck. And not an ounce of spare flesh was on his long lean frame.

"Which one of you is the sheriff?" Linda demanded, coming quickly to the point after her gaze had whipped over all three men.

By this time each was fully standing. The older man shifted his weight. "I am. What's the problem?"

Melanie stayed behind Linda. Under normal circumstances she didn't like crowds, preferring instead to take people on one at a time. Linda felt her hovering presence and thrust her own personality forward to protect her.

"My sister and I have come to take possession of a claim. But when we found it, two men were already there. They drew a gun and shot at us."

"Are you sure you were in the right place?" the older man asked.

"I'm positive."

The sheriff relaxed against his desk, smiling at her kindly. "It's pretty easy to be mistaken out here. Has happened more than once."

"It wasn't a mistake!" Linda denied. She didn't like the way he was belittling their problem.

"You've been here before?" he asked.

"Not until today."

"Well then?"

"We have directions...and we got further directions from the man at the gas station across the street. He said he knew our uncle and where his claim was located."

The sandy-haired deputy laughed. "Well, there's your problem then."

The older man's smile increased as well. "Sure is. Old Jason thinks he knows everything. But he gets confused sometimes."

"He wasn't confused this time," Linda replied, gritting the words through her teeth. "And if he was, even if we both were, doesn't it mean anything to you that those men *shot* at us?"

The sheriff shook his head. "Not particularly. People around here take a keen interest in protecting what they've got. You don't just go up to them and start asking questions."

"It's *our* claim!" Linda said stubbornly.

The taller man spoke. He pushed the chair behind him back against the wall, out of the way. "Maybe she knows what she's talking about, Patrick. It wouldn't hurt to take a look."

"Just what I was thinking. But it's still not out of the ordinary to get a potshot taken at you when you're trespassing. You should know that, Tate."

Melanie spoke for the first time. "We have papers proving our ownership...wouldn't they indicate the proper location?"

Everyone turned to look at her, including Linda. She hadn't thought of that. She smiled at her sister, who smiled shyly back.

"That's right," she confirmed, twisting back to face the men. "My sister's right."

Melanie retrieved the papers from her purse. "Here," she said quietly.

The man called Patrick took them from her, but when he read the name registered on the claim, he had no need to check a map. "You're Roger Conway's relatives." He looked up, frowning. "Why didn't you say that?"

"I thought I had," Linda returned.

The sheriff shook his head. "There has to be some kind of misunderstanding. Tate, Roland, why don't you two accompany these ladies to the site and see what you can find out?"

"They're claim jumpers," Linda said firmly.

The sandy-haired man grinned. "Come on, Tate. Let's go catch us some *claim jumpers*."

He wasn't taking them seriously. Neither was the older man. But the tall deputy, Tate, didn't seem as skeptical. It was to him that Linda gave a short assenting nod.

Chapter Three

Linda and Melanie followed the Jeep with the insignia of the sheriff's department on the door all the way back to the disputed claim. The deputies had asked if they wanted to ride with them, but Linda had quickly declined, not wishing to lose any measure of independence. If by chance they were proved wrong, she didn't want to have to go through the ordeal of being enclosed in the car with them all the way back to town.

As had happened twice before, the two sisters pushed through the brush to the stream. This time they were following the men—and Linda couldn't say that she wanted it any other way. A man with a gun might not hesitate to threaten two unarmed women, but he would think twice about challenging two deputies.

The little procession stopped at the edge of the clearing, all eyes searching for signs of encroachment. But only the bubbling water and twittering birds could be seen and heard.

"This the place you came to before?" the taller deputy asked.

Linda nodded. "This is it."

The deputies moved across a narrow board spanning the stream. One of them called out to anyone who might be there, but no one answered.

Linda and Melanie glanced at each other.

The sandy-haired deputy walked to the lean-to and went inside. He soon came out again. "No one's home," he said.

They continued to look around, going a little farther afield. Finally they recrossed the stream to where the women waited. Silence met their arrival.

"They *were* here," Linda said.

The blond deputy sniggered. "Looks like they left, then."

Tate ignored his companion. "They probably got spooked. Decided to cut their losses and run. They weren't planning on you two showing up." He turned away, his gaze going over the stream and the work area. "You planning to stay here and work this place?"

Linda's back was rigid. They had been made to look like fools, which was not a productive way to start a new venture. "Yes."

"Know anything about working a claim?"

"Enough."

"Ever done it before?" His gaze swung back to Linda, the dark eyes narrowed assessingly.

She lifted her chin and decided to take charge of the situation. They owed these men nothing, not even an explanation. They were deputies; aiding people was their job. She extended her hand. "Thank you for coming to help us. I'm sorry it turned out to be a waste of time."

"What if the men come back?" Tate questioned. He didn't make a reciprocal motion.

Linda felt Melanie move restively beside her.

The deputy continued, "There's a boardinghouse in town that's clean, affordable."

"I can vouch for that," Roland stated. "And they have good food. Owner's wife is a great cook."

"You could stay there until you're sure things are safe here," Tate added.

Linda weighed good sense against the lightness of their pockets. She motioned to the lean-to. "We'll stay here, thanks. I think you're right. We probably scared them off."

"Place isn't very comfortable."

"We'll still stay here."

The dark-haired deputy shrugged. "If that's what you want..."

"It is."

The sandy-haired man ran a palm down his jeans leg and reached for the hand that Linda had let fall back to her side. "My name's Roland Barns. This here's Tate Winslow." He indicated the other man with a jerk of his head. "You have to excuse Tate. He comes from a big city... he's always expecting bad things to happen out here in the country."

"I grew up here, Roland."

"Cities have a way of messing up your mind," Roland continued, as if the other man had not spoken. "Live in 'em for a few years and you get warped. Forget how to trust your fellowman."

"Some fellowmen should never be trusted," Tate suggested.

The wide smile that had been on Roland's face stiffened slightly. "Well," he said, "that's true. Some more than others, I suppose. But then I'm just an ignorant country boy. Never been to college. Much less teach at one."

Linda frowned, feeling as if she had stepped into the middle of an argument without being aware of it. A tension existed between the two men—one she didn't understand but definitely sensed.

Tate Winslow's dark eyes were fixed on his companion. He made no reply. Instead, he turned again to the two sisters. "At least let us help you get settled. I'm sure you have things in your car that need to be brought over."

Under other circumstances Linda would have refused. But with Melanie as weak as she was, she consented. Without assistance, her sister would insist upon helping and weaken herself even more.

Three trips took care of transporting everything—a sad commentary on the paltriness of their belongings. Over the past two months, their individual possessions had been cut to the bone and almost everything else sold. They had retained only the bare essentials—and the ranch. So far.

Neither man commented on the sparsity of their belongings; they had no idea that this was everything. To them, the sisters might be on a lark, a few weeks of fun spent in an unusual occupation, not making a desperate attempt at salvation.

"The lean-to might need a little clearing out," Tate said as he straightened from placing a box on the bank.

"We'll take care of it," Linda answered.

"The men might have left it in a mess."

"So you believe there *were* men?"

"You said there were. I believe you."

"Your partner doesn't."

"He's not my partner."

Linda glanced at Melanie, who was being assisted across the stream by the man they were talking about. The color was high in her sister's cheeks, and Linda wondered what the deputy had been saying to her.

"We'll be just fine." She turned back to Tate Winslow. "Don't worry about us. We're accustomed to making do."

"Your sister seems to tire easily."

He was observant. "She's been ill."

"This is a pretty tough life. You going to stay here long?"

"Long enough," Linda replied. She was reaching for the box in which they had packed some cleansers and kitchen utensils—they hadn't been sure just what state their uncle's place would be in—when she heard the man standing next to her give a low chuckle.

She glanced up and saw that his handsome face was lighted by a half-amused smile. "You sure like to keep things close," he said.

"Maybe I learned that the hard way," she clipped.

The dark eyes narrowed with interest, but before he could make another comment, Roland Barns came up to them and slapped him on the back. From his expression, Tate Winslow didn't appreciate the familiarity.

"We should be headed back to town, don't you think, Tate? Can't spend all day talking to pretty ladies—much as we'd like to."

Tate moved slightly, so that the other man's hand fell away. Linda noticed the action, even if Roland didn't. When she looked at him, he seemed blithely unaware, but she wasn't sure if he was putting on an act. Many of the things the man said and did seemed like an act. Either that or flamboyancy was an integral part of his personality.

Tate spoke to the two women as Melanie came to stand at Linda's side. "If you two need help, don't hesitate to contact us. One of us will probably stop by every once in a while...just to see that things are going all right."

"Do you do that at all the claims?" Linda challenged. It had been a long time since anyone had offered to look out for them, to care for their well-being. But she couldn't easily accept this man's offer. The habits fallen into while being assailed over the past few months were difficult to break. She could accept some forms of help, but not patronization.

"We like to keep an eye on things," he returned. "Patrick always has."

"Patrick?" Melanie queried.

"Patrick McHenry. The sheriff. He's a good man, takes his job seriously."

Linda bit back the opinion that he hadn't seemed to take their situation very seriously. But possibly she hadn't given him a fair chance. They had rushed into his office to demand immediate help, and he might not be the type of person to jump into things without understanding the entire picture.

"And pretty ladies are a lot easier to look at than our usual grizzly old prospectors," Roland unhelpfully broke in.

Both Linda and Tate threw him an irritated look.

"Come on, let's go," Tate murmured after a moment, his tone impatient.

"Goodbye... and thank you," Melanie called after them, her voice soft, sweet.

Each man turned to give a short wave. Linda's hands stayed tightly at her sides. She hoped never to have to call upon either one of them again.

Melanie watched the two men move out of view, then glanced at her sister. "It was nice of them to help us, wasn't it?" she asked.

Linda nodded.

"You didn't like them?" Melanie guessed.

"Not particularly." Linda picked up the box she had reached for earlier, balancing its heavy load upon her hip. The sooner she got started with the cleanup, the sooner they could get settled in.

Melanie followed her inside the shelter. "Do you think the claim jumpers will be back?"

"I hope not."

Melanie shivered in the shadowed room, whether from the sudden change in temperature or from the grubby mess either the men or their uncle had left. Bits and pieces of rubbish were scattered all about the place, along with various pieces of oddly shaped equipment. Boxes of all sizes were everywhere, some with their contents spilling out in a confused jumble.

Linda sighed as she surveyed the room.

"What will we do if they *do* come back?" Melanie asked, her voice wavery.

Linda knew that if her sister had her choice, they would return to Nevada and the ranch they were about to lose and try to pretend that none of this had happened—that none of it *was* happening. She took pity on her younger sibling, drawing an arm around her thin shoulders, pulling her close.

"Everything's going to be all right. It will all work out. I told you that it would, and it will. I promise."

"But—"

"No buts. All we have to do is concentrate on one thing: find as much gold as we can, as quickly as we can." *It's our only hope,* she almost added, but censored the words. Melanie had been through enough for one day. A reminder of their dilemma would do her little good. Although Linda knew that the situation was never far from either of their minds, she also knew that dwelling on the matter had no merit. Only time and hard work—not to mention luck—could resolve their predicament.

She hugged her sister once again and forced a smile. "Hey, this place isn't so bad. When the lawyer said there was a lean-to, I thought it was going to be a shack. This is almost a cabin! We can make this into a nice place to stay." At least they wouldn't be left without a home of some sort if they lost the ranch.

Melanie muffled a sniff and blinked the tears, a sign of weakness, away from her eyes. "No, it's not so bad."

Linda's smile held. "Here. Why don't you find our coffeepot and make us some coffee, while I . . . while I check what's in some of these boxes?"

"I wish I wasn't so tired."

"Don't worry about it," Linda answered with fierce love for her sister. "You can't help it and you get stronger every day." That was a lie. Melanie wasn't getting stronger, which was another thing to worry about.

"Are you hungry?" Melanie asked. "I could make us sandwiches from what we have left in the cooler."

"Great," Linda replied.

As her sister moved away, Linda's eyes followed her. And in their pale blue depths were the deepening shadows of quiet desperation.

TATE WINSLOW stood at the edge of the crumbling graveyard that was tucked away in a small hollow on the outskirts of Amador Springs. For as many years as he could remember, this particular spot had been abandoned—the new cemetery had been placed on the other side of town. Weeds had grown up to vie for supremacy with the old tombstones. And when the moon was full, wisps of memory seemed to take shape and float above the forgotten field until dispersed by the morning sun.

As a child he had come here often, both by day and by night. Here people didn't judge, because they had already been judged themselves. And to them, the quiet coming and going of a lonely child might have been a comfort.

Headstones with dates from the previous century had kept him company, as well as fostering curiosity about the past. He had read the names and epitaphs over and over again, wondering about their lives, weaving dreams of bygone days.

To him, the cemetery had been a magical place...a land where his father would never come. Not even in his most drunken state. To Dan Winslow there had been no goodness in the place, only superstition, which had meant that for hours on end Tate could escape the harshness of his life.

Tate scuffed a stone with the tip of his hiking shoe and adjusted his hand's position against a low-riding oak tree limb. He didn't like to remember. But he had been doing little else since his return to Amador Springs. Memory and people would allow him little else. He was Dan Winslow's boy. Forever young, forever needy.

Tate momentarily shut his eyes, turning away from the pain.

He had been surprised by how little the town had changed. The population had been reduced, but that wasn't unusual in a place so far removed from the hub of life. The wood- and rock-faced buildings had remained the same. The dust, the pack of hungry dogs jostling among themselves on the sidewalks, the business names etched on each plate glass window.

Tate thought of Miriam, thought of where the two of them might have spent the summer. What was he doing here? Why had he allowed himself to be held hostage by his past?

Immediately he had his answer: *Patrick*.

Tate moved away from the tree, stepping past the silent companions of his youth. Patrick was the one who had shocked him. Beneath the man's slightly corpulent descent into advancing age had been fear. And Tate had never before seen the man afraid.

"I don't know what I'm going to do, Tate. People are upset. They...I know there's rumors going around, saying I'm too old, that I should resign. But I can't *do* that, Tate. I can't! Being sheriff here is all the life I've ever really known. It would be like—like cutting off both my arms." In his eyes was a pleading look that had wrenched at Tate's heart. "Things have been happening...strange things. And I haven't been able to come up with a solution. I need someone on my side, Tate. Someone I can trust."

That was how he had become a deputy. Even though Patrick already had a deputy in Roland Barns.

Someone I can trust. The words continued to bother Tate. Did Patrick not trust Roland Barns? And if he didn't, why not? His old friend had confided no more, asking him instead to keep a steady watch.

Roland Barns was the type of man that Tate had little use for. Three-quarters bombast, the remaining quarter unknown. Roland Barns was easy to read on the surface, but there was something beneath that surface that nagged at Tate. Did it nag at Patrick, as well?

Eventually, when he had examined the problem from all sides and come to a tentative conclusion, he would talk again with Patrick. Until then, he would continue to keep his counsel as Patrick wished—telling everyone in town that he had merely come back for a visit and decided to stay on temporarily to assist his old friend.

Roland Barns had pretended to welcome him, seemingly not in the least bothered by an addition to the team. But he never let an opportunity pass to insert a subtle dig, such as those he had used earlier when they were helping the two women.

Roland's comments were always difficult to challenge, because of the times he chose to make them as well as the craftsmanship of their delivery. Usually he left a person unsure of his motives, and sometimes unsure if the digs had even been made deliberately.

Tate brought the engine of his car to life after resettling into his seat. The women. Two sisters. Alike and yet unalike. One was quiet and soft—the other harder, more aggressive.

He frowned as he thought of the men they said had shot at them. As Patrick had told them, such an occurrence wasn't all that unusual here, where people tended to be very protective of what they owned—and what they hoped to find. This wouldn't be the first time claim jumpers had tried to prove their right of possession with a weapon. Many of the epitaphs in the old cemetery attested to how violent life had been and still could be. But put together with the other occurences of the past months, it did give him a moment of pause. Were the events somehow related?

Tate shifted gears and looked over his shoulder as he backed the car down the narrow lane. He had taken a break for lunch and had come instead to the cemetery. He was due back at the office to relieve Patrick. Roland, thankfully, had something planned for that afternoon. He wouldn't be subjected to conversation with him for hours on end as they shared the tiny room.

The drive to the center of town was short, barely five minutes. But then Amador Springs could be traversed on foot in a little over ten. Tate parked his car in the side lot and stepped onto the wooden sidewalk that fronted the office. His steps sounded hollow in the afternoon quiet.

As he opened the door, he was preparing to utter a teasing aside to his friend when he saw that the office was occupied by someone besides Patrick. A woman was there. Middle-aged, plump, with curly brown hair worn short to her head. She was livid.

"And I don't plan to leave until you come up with something! My father disappears and no one seems to care! What kind of sheriff are you?"

"We care, Mrs. Armbruster. We care a great deal." Patrick's words were conciliatory. "But it's not all that unusual for a prospector to just pick up and leave. I don't require everyone to report to me...to tell me exactly what they're doing, where they're going. People wouldn't stand for it, especially not these people. I'm sure your father just moved on to another place, and that you'll be hearing from him soon."

"He didn't tell me he was leaving," the woman returned stubbornly. "And he always tells me what he's planning to do, because he knows I worry about him."

"I'm sure it will all work out. But just to put your mind at rest, my deputies and I will ask around."

"A search party would be more appropriate."

Patrick glanced at Tate for the first time since the younger man entered the room.

"This is one of my deputies now, Mrs. Armbruster. Tate Winslow."

The woman turned furious eyes on him. She looked him up and down, didn't seem impressed and immediately turned back to the sheriff. "Just don't you forget. I'm not going to leave until you produce some information. I want you to find my father—and I want you to find him *now*!"

With that she marched from the office, closing the door behind her with unnecessary force.

Patrick winced.

Tate leaned back against the desk behind him and folded his arms over his chest. "Trouble?" he asked. The answer was self-evident, but he knew that Patrick needed a nudge to start talking. Otherwise he might sit for hours in a solitary slump, saying nothing, with a heavy frown furrowing his brow.

Patrick looked up. "You could say that. You heard?"

Tate nodded. "What do you think happened to him?"

Patrick sighed. "God only knows. Might have moved on, like I said... or something else."

The last three words hung on the air. "You think this might be connected with the other disappearances?"

Patrick nodded. "Sometimes I wonder if I shouldn't resign. I don't seem to be much use to anyone anymore."

"Don't say that. Don't even think it," Tate said sharply, responding to the gruff anguish in his friend's voice. "If you resign, who'd take your place?"

"Roland?"

"And you think he'd do a better job?"

Patrick shrugged.

Tate tried another track. "How many people have disappeared now?"

"Three."

"And none of them said anything to you, to anyone, about changing stakes?"

"Not one. One day they were on their claim—the next they weren't. No one thought anything about it at first."

"And haven't people just disappeared in the past?"

"You know they have."

"And they turned up again, too, didn't they?"

"You know the answer to that, as well."

"So what makes you think this time is any different?"

Patrick rubbed his forehead, concentrating on the area between his eyebrows. "Just a feeling I have. Intuition from all the years I've been doing this job. Something about this doesn't smell right."

"But you heard the woman, she's a worrier."

"Wait until she hears the rumors."

Tate's mouth tightened. *The rumors.* Hard to pin down; hard to discredit. His gaze went over Patrick, the man who had single-handedly changed the course of his life.

He hadn't been required to do what he had done. Saving a child from destruction hadn't been a part of his job description. But omissions like that had never hindered Patrick McHenry. If something needed doing, he did it—no matter the inconvenience to himself. Had the people of Amador Springs forgotten that? Tate was sure that he was not the only person Patrick had helped over the years.

Tate moved his arm and felt the unfamiliar pressure of the deputy sheriff's badge that was pinned to his shirt. Ever since Patrick had given it to him, he had felt a fraud. He was no lawman, no enforcer of public order. The badge had as little force behind it as a piece of costume jewelry. Yet he seemed the only person willing to take up Patrick's cause.

"To hell with the rumors!" he said shortly, hoping to dispel the depression that was engulfing the man who had done so much to help him.

A slow smile began to tug at the crop of short white whiskers on either side of Patrick's mouth. "That sounds more like the old Tate than the new one. You used to say to hell with everything."

"Now I'm more selective," Tate returned.

Patrick's gray eyes crinkled and for the first time since Tate's arrival, he looked more like the person he used to be: filled with a quiet command of himself and of the situation. Then the smile slowly disappeared. He stood up. "Well, I'm turning it over to you now, son. Call me if anything happens."

"I will," Tate promised.

He watched as his friend moved to the door. Patrick walked as if something hurt... and Tate wondered if the cause was physical or emotional. For the townspeople to doubt him was the cruelest blow that could have been delivered. Patrick had given his life to Amador Springs. He had never married; the town was his wife, its inhabitants were his children. And now, as the uncaring finger of old age was fast upon him, he was not being allowed to reap the contentment that should have been his.

"Patrick," Tate called as the older man crossed the threshold to the sidewalk. "Everything's going to work out."

Patrick turned back to look at him. He hesitated. "Sure," he said, his reply soft. "Sure it will."

Then he was gone and only the echo of his words remained.

Chapter Four

Linda awakened to the sound of birds calling their enjoyment of morning. Sunlight filtered in through cracks in the lean-to's frame, and she had to move so that she wouldn't be blinded. At first she didn't remember where she was, looking about the crowded room in puzzlement. Then memory returned, and she groaned lightly to herself as she let her head fall back against her sleeping bag.

It had taken her forever to go to sleep last night. Melanie had slept almost instantly, exhaustion taking it's toll. Linda had tossed and turned, aware of each and every sound that broke the silence around their shelter—afraid that the men would come back, afraid that she had made the wrong decision. What was money where safety was concerned? They had a little stake; they could have spent one night in town. But as the hours passed and nothing came to shatter their tenuous security, she had eventually given in to her own exhaustion.

Not far away Melanie stirred. The night had been cold. Linda had spread the extra blanket they'd brought from home over her sister's sleeping bag, providing extra warmth. For herself, she had looked at one of the blankets left by either her uncle or the men and decided just to be a little cool. She didn't want to use very much of anything until she had the chance to air it out and inspect it more closely.

Melanie made a soft sound as she awakened, one of questioning fear.

Linda immediately sat up. "Good morning," she said, pushing the hair away from her face and straightening her rumpled clothing. She presented a smiling face to her sister's look of dismay.

"I'd hoped it was all a dream," Melanie whispered.

"Nope. We're here. How'd you sleep?"

"I don't remember anything after I lay down." She rubbed the muscles of her lower back. "How about you?"

"I slept great. Like a log. I just woke up a few minutes ago."

Melanie stood up, wavering slightly before gaining a firm footing. She looked around the room. Linda hadn't gotten very far yesterday evening in clearing out the mess. She had only been able to straighten a few boxes... and had found that those contained all sorts of odd bits and pieces of their uncle's life. He had been a veritable pack rat, keeping everything with an almost obsessive vengeance: letters and bills, along with balls of string, stubs of candles and broken utensils.

Melanie sighed. "It's going to take us weeks just to go through this."

Linda pushed to her feet, shaking her head. "No. I've decided we're just going to stack it to one side and forget about it... at least for now."

"But what about all those pieces of machinery?"

Linda frowned then dismissed them. "We'll put them outside. Heaven knows if they're any good, or if Uncle Roger decided to keep them because he liked the way they looked."

"Crazy Uncle Roger."

Linda smiled slightly in response. In the night, in a weak moment, she had wondered if Uncle Roger really had been crazy and made up his story of finding gold. The lawyer had only his word for it. There had been nothing to show.

"Are you hungry?" Linda asked, hoping to divert her sister's attention.

Melanie shrugged. "Not really."

"Well, I am. How about lighting the camp stove? I'll see what I can rustle up." She found their box of supplies. It was pitifully inadequate. "Maybe we should go into town sometime today and get a few more things."

"Whatever you think," Melanie answered.

Linda shot her sister a careful look. Melanie was paler today than she had been yesterday. She quelled another onslaught of fear. "You can take first call in the outhouse," she offered.

Melanie shuddered. "I don't like it in there. It doesn't smell good, and I'm afraid there're spiders."

Linda agreed. "When we're in town we'll get some lime and some bug spray. Will that help?"

Melanie nodded. "I suppose."

When she was alone, Linda's busy fingers stopped and her eyes closed. *Please let there be gold,* she asked whichever deity might be willing to look kindly upon them for a change. *Don't let all this be for nothing.*

Sometimes she felt so helpless, so trapped. They had one more opportunity to rescue their lives. If that didn't work...

Her shoulders stiffened as she set them firmly and resumed her work. They would not let this opportunity slip away without a fight. They had to have good luck. They had to.

TATE ROLLED DOWN the Jeep's window as the heat of day overtook the chill of night. Since early that morning he, Patrick and Roland had been making inquiries of the far-flung prospectors in the area. Each had taken a different route, and all were to meet back in town to correlate what they had learned.

For himself, he had learned nothing. No one knew anything of the missing prospectors, and most seemed irritated that they were being asked once again. Each expected the law, namely Patrick, to discover if there'd been any foul play, but no one wanted to discuss the matter. Solitary men, and a few women, bent on only one course: wringing from the land the greatest amount of gold in the shortest possible amount of time. Not that many would ever find their fortune, though years were spent in looking.

Tate remembered his father and all the men he had lived around while growing up. The search for gold was eternal; the goal eternally elusive. Color would be found, decent quantities would be taken, but rarely in the amounts most people dreamed of.

Prospectors were a closemouthed group. And now that the price of gold had skyrocketed, they were even more self-protective. Especially around anyone connected with the law. They didn't want anyone knowing what was going on with their claims. Heightened paranoia about any form of police intrusion tightened their lips even more.

Tate had heard the rumors that more gold was being found...that some of the prospectors were beginning to realize a good reward for their patience and hard work. Sometimes when one had too much to drink, words would slip.

And he knew all about the loose words of people who lost control of their drinking. He had lived with it from the time he first remembered to his eighteenth birthday, when he shook the dust of Amador Springs off his newly purchased shoes—bought with Patrick's aid, of course—and left his father to his fate, while he struggled to form a fate of his own.

He shook his head, trying to force the memories back into oblivion. When things couldn't be changed, they were best left alone. That was a philosophy he had come to nurture. And so far, it had held him in good stead.

Tate noticed where he was on the road back to town and glanced at his watch. He was early and had time to stop. He drew the Jeep to a halt in the small clearing. When he stepped outside, he stretched his long frame. Hours spent behind a desk did little to prepare a body for more active work. Getting to some of the claims was difficult. Not rope and piton work, but rugged all the same.

He started through the brush toward the embankment and paused beside the gnarled old oak. Only one of the women was working. The other was sitting in the shade of a group of trees.

For several seconds he merely watched. Then, finally, he moved forward.

LINDA HAD SPREAD the blankets she'd found in the shelter over the branches of some nearby brush. Next she had begun the job of transporting the bits and pieces of equipment outside. Finally, when that was done, her attention had returned to the sun-warmed blankets that she began to shake, remembering the times she had seen her mother do the very same thing with the blankets the wranglers had used at the bunkhouse. In a way it felt good to be doing something her mother had done, but the action was also tinged with sadness. Her mother had died when she was barely ten. All she had of her was a little girl's memories. But she was thankful for that, at least, because Melanie's memories were even less formed.

Wrapping a blanket over her arm, she walked to where Melanie was sitting. Her sister had insisted upon helping, so she had devised a plan to keep her at rest, while also allowing her to assist.

She was just preparing to give her sister the first blanket to fold and stack, when footsteps on the other side of the stream caused her to jerk around, her heart leaping to her throat.

Reflexively she expected to see the men from yesterday. But the long, lean form of the deputy met her vision, and she released her breath with a quick rush of relief. Typically, though, after a fright, her next reaction was aggravation.

"Are you trying to scare us to death?" she demanded. "Hasn't anyone ever told you you should announce your presence when you come up on people unawares?"

He stopped short, surprised by her vehemence. Then a slow smile creased the sides of his cheeks and his dark eyes crinkled at the corners. He nodded to Melanie before concentrating fully on Linda.

"Well, since there wasn't a door, I couldn't knock."

"You could have said something."

"Like what? Hello, I'm here...don't jump out of your skin?"

Linda looked away even as her mouth twitched in irritation—with herself, with the situation. She always seemed to step off on the wrong foot and look foolish.

Melanie took up the slack caused by Linda's withdrawal. "How nice to see you...Tate. Isn't that your name?"

He nodded, his gaze moving slowly from Linda's stony profile to her sister's more welcoming expression. "I dropped by to see how you were doing. To check if you've seen any more of those two men."

Linda's head snapped around. "We're perfectly all right."

He glanced around the site. "Looks like you're making some progress."

Melanie smiled self-effacingly. "Linda is. I'm practically useless."

"No, you're not," Linda quickly denied.

Her sister looked at her. "You're doing all the work."

"You're helping."

Tate Winslow shifted position, uncomfortable in a situation he knew nothing about. He brought the subject back to the reason for his visit. "I've been out talking with other prospectors this morning and while I was there, I asked if anyone had seen any strangers."

"And?" Linda prompted.

He shook his head. "No one has." She drew a quick breath, but before she could speak, he said, "That's doesn't mean they aren't here. It just means no one's seen them but you."

"Small comfort," she clipped.

"Small enough," he agreed.

Linda could feel her sister's censure. Melanie had always been more devoted to manners than she. To Linda, manners were important, but not necessarily—or always—expedient.

Melanie smiled again. "We do thank you for the trouble you've gone to, and for stopping by." She paused, glanced at Linda, then deliberately added, "Would you like to have lunch with us? Nothing special, just some beans and canned chili."

Linda's body tensed. She didn't want him to eat lunch with them. She didn't want to have to pretend to be jolly in front of a stranger, even if the stranger was trying to do them a favor.

Tate started to shake his head as he glanced at his watch. "I wish I could, but I have to be back in town soon."

"We wouldn't want to keep you," Linda broke in, possibly a little too quickly.

Tate Winslow met her gaze across the stream and another slow smile crossed his features. "But on second thought," he said, "I do need to eat. If it wouldn't be too much trouble..."

Passages of Gold 53

"No trouble at all," Melanie answered. "I'll get right on it. At least that's something I *can* do."

Linda was aware of her sister moving toward the lean-to. She was also aware that she was stuck with their visitor... with egg on her face. She knew he had accepted because she had shown such ill grace. Her hand flicked at her side. "You might as well come on over then," she said, as close to conceding defeat as she was likely to get.

Wisely Tate made no reply. Instead, he made his way across the narrow board that spanned the gurgling water.

Linda shifted her hands to the back pockets of her jeans and rocked once back and forth, from her toes to the heels of her boots and back again. She tried to look anywhere but at him. Finally curiosity got the better of her, and she shot him a glance out of the corner of her eye. He wasn't looking at her. Rather, he was interested in some of the equipment she had dragged outside. He moved closer to inspect one object more thoroughly, hunching down beside it.

"Haven't seen one like this in years," he remarked. He glanced at her then back at the object. "It's an old rocker. Where'd you find it?"

Linda came a few steps closer to peer at the wooden object. "Inside the lean-to."

He gave the object a push and it began to rock from side to side like a baby's cradle. "Do you know what this is?" he asked.

Linda shrugged. "Not really."

"It's practically an antique. From the looks of it, it *is* an antique. It's something prospectors used to wash for gold in. They'd take the rock and gravel they were interested in and put it in here—" He indicated the opening on top. "Then they'd rock it to sift it through these riffle bars—" he ran his fingers over the wooden slats nailed in parallel lines across the section below. "—and that would catch the gold. The Forty-Niners used them a lot."

He had captured Linda's interest. "Did they find a lot of gold that way?" she asked.

"I suppose so."

Tate saw the intensity with which she was studying the old rocker. "Of course, if they'd had some of the equipment people use today, no telling how much more they'd have brought out."

"You mean they'd have gotten it all?"

Gone was Linda's antagonistic response to the man. For the moment, he was telling her something she needed to know. The pamphlet she had picked up at the library hadn't told her all that much.

He laughed. "No need to worry about that. People could probably wash bedrock here for the next five hundred years and still not find all of it. More keeps filtering in all the time."

"Where does it come from?"

"From the land all around. It washes out with the rains...natural erosion...." Tate stood up, causing her to take a step back. He frowned as he asked, "Just how much do you know about looking for gold?"

"I know enough," she lied.

"You didn't know what this was." He motioned to the rocker.

"I thought you said that was used in the past."

"Nothing to keep people from using one today. Some probably do. What worked then can work now."

"Economics."

"What?"

"Economics." She lifted her head, brazening her way through. "We have better ways today."

"Name a couple."

Linda searched her mind. Words with little meaning were recalled from the pamphlet's text. She grasped for one. "Dredging."

He nodded, still suspicious.

She clung to her correct guess. "That's what we're going to do. We're going to dredge."

"You've done it before?"

She couldn't lie again. He might ask her to prove it by showing him. "I'm sure it's not that hard."

"So you haven't. Somehow I didn't think so."

"I can learn."

"You ever panned?"

She was on safer ground. This was something she had understood from the pamphlet. The idea of taking sand and gravel in a shallow pan and sloshing water over it, until only the gold remained, was what had convinced her that they could make a success of coming here. With a little practice, she knew that she could get good at it. If other people could, she could.

"Not in actual fact, no, but I'm a quick learner."

He merely looked at her. Finally he gave a little laugh. "You've got guts, lady."

"Thank you." She took a breath, regaining her confidence. "Now if we're through with the quiz..."

He laughed softly again. "Once a teacher, always a teacher," he mused.

"What did you say?"

"Nothing important."

At that moment, Melanie stuck her head out of the lean-to door and told them that lunch was served.

In the end they took their filled bowls outside. It was cooler and not as confining as trying to crush the three of them into one room. For that small suggestion from her sister, Linda was inordinately grateful.

TATE WAS a few minutes late arriving back in town. Patrick and Roland were already in the office. Roland, his feet propped up on the front of Patrick's desk, greeted him with a sarcastic, "Did you get lost? I know you grew up around here, but things do change...sometimes a lot."

Tate held back the words he wanted to say to the man, a practice that was becoming increasingly difficult. He didn't like the little barbs, the almost incomprehensible innuendo.

"I stopped by the Conway claim. I wanted to see if the men had come back to bother them."

Roland sat up, drawing his feet to the floor. The smile that twisted his lips was mocking. "And to catch a look at some prime tail? I don't blame you. I might stop by there later myself."

"They're coming into town." Tate had a sudden aversion to Roland going out to the womens' claim.

Roland's smile widened. "Good. I'll keep an eye out for 'em."

Tate stood stiffly, wishing that he had said nothing.

Patrick cleared his throat. "I think we'd better get back to the business at hand. Any news, Tate?"

Tate shifted his attention to the older man. "Nothing. No one's seen anything, heard anything."

"Same with us." Patrick rubbed his shaggy head. He sighed deeply. "Got to be something we're missing," he said almost to himself.

"You have an idea?" Tate asked.

"Wish I did, son. Wish I did. I just..."

Roland scraped his chair against the floor. "Hope you don't mind if I get out of here a little early. We've taken care of all that we can for today, right?"

Patrick's gray eyes were tired as he looked across at his deputy. "Sure. You go ahead."

Roland swaggered to the door. Then he turned, giving Tate one parting shot. "Gotta be sure to catch the ladies. Don't want to miss an opportunity to have a little fun."

Tate's expression remained impassive until Roland Barns was completely out of the room. Then, frowning darkly, he said, "You know, he's the type who really starts to get under your skin. The longer you know him, the more irritating he becomes, until finally you just want to..."

Patrick laughed. "He's just egging you on, Tate. He's relatively harmless."

"Do you really believe that?"

Patrick was a few seconds replying. "I'm not sure what I believe anymore." He was silent again, but Tate could sense that there was more to come. Then he murmured quietly, "Mrs. Armbruster paid us another call before you got here. She's heard the rumors."

"And is in a suitable frame of mind—dammit, Patrick!"

"We can't blame her, son. She's got a right to be concerned."

"She doesn't have the right to be obnoxious. Why doesn't she just wait and let you do your job?"

Patrick stood up. He didn't answer the question. Instead he said, "I'm going to get a bite to eat. You want me to bring you something?"

Tate murmured a refusal.

As his old friend left the room, striving desperately to present a brave front, a helpless anger blazed through Tate. An anger like none he had experienced since childhood.

MELANIE WAS nearly through giving her lecture. It had started almost the moment following Tate Winslow's departure from the claim and had continued, sporadically because she would tire, almost all the way into town. Linda glanced at her sister and saw the spark that had lighted in her eyes. She held her tongue. If being rude to someone would bring that much animation to Melanie's spirits, she would take every opportunity she could find to be rude to someone again. She gave a secret smile, one she carefully hid.

"I've apologized. What more can I do?" she asked, playing along with her sister's line of complaint.

"I think you should apologize to him. Honestly, Linda, the man is just trying to help."

"He thinks he knows everything."

"He probably does. At least—" she reconsidered "—he knows more about finding gold than we do."

"I still don't think we should have agreed to let him come out tomorrow."

"He's going to help us get started. What's wrong with that?"

"Oh, nothing." Linda grimaced.

"I saw the way you looked just now. What is it with you, Linda? He seems a very nice man."

"I didn't say he wasn't nice."

Melanie sighed and let her head fall back against the rear cushion of the seat. "I don't want to talk about it anymore. In the end you'll do exactly as you want. You always do."

Linda glanced at her sister. Was that a tinge of resentment she'd heard in Melanie's voice? "I'll be nice. Okay?" she promised. "And I'll apologize."

A soft smile touched Melanie's lips.

LINDA DIRECTED the car into a parking spot in front of the general store. It, too, looked like something straight from a Western movie. All it needed was several horses tied to a hitching post rather than spaces for cars. The nearest town to the ranch where she and Melanie had grown up had long turned its back on the past and was doing everything it could to catch up with the modern world. A movie theater was next door to a video game room, a booming real estate office shared the same sidewalk with a thriving restaurant. Coming to Amador Springs was like taking a leap back in time.

Linda stepped from the car but leaned back before leaving. "Are you sure you want to stay here?" she asked. "I might be awhile."

Melanie smiled slightly. "I know. I'll be fine."

Linda silently tapped a finger on the warm metal of the car's roof. Then she turned away, a troubled frown marking her expression.

In the end, she was even longer in the store than she had thought. The owner, a woman in her mid-fifties, loved to talk. She went on and on, covering just about everything, barely giving Linda a chance to break in. Finally, though, she was able to make an excuse and hurry away with her arms full of two grocery sacks.

She had been concerned about Melanie sitting in the hot car. But when she arrived at the car, Melanie was no longer inside. Linda's frown deepened as she started to search the area around her. It was then she saw the deputy with the sandy mustache waving from across the road.

"If you're looking for your sister, I brought her in here," he called, jerking a thumb to the café behind him. Through a dusty window, Linda could see Melanie give a weak wave.

Linda deposited the bags in the car and hurried across the street. Roland Barns escorted her into the café. He continued speaking. "She was feeling the heat, so I brought her in here to cool off. Got her something to drink."

Linda murmured her thanks and closed the short distance to her sister. She slid into the chair next to her. "Are you all right?" she asked.

"I'm fine," Melanie responded. She glanced at the deputy and said softly but with muted feeling, "I told him I was all right."

Roland cut in. "You didn't look all right. So I did my duty and took care of the problem." He grinned. "Now you can't say that cold drink didn't taste good."

Melanie forced a tiny smile. "No, that's true. I can't."

Linda stood up, pulling Melanie with her. "Well, the best thing we can do is get back to the claim and make an early night of it."

"I was going to ask if the two of you would like to have dinner with me. This place—" he motioned to the tiny café "—isn't exactly beautiful, but..."

Linda shook her head. "No. Thank you. I think we should go back."

His eyelashes were as pale as his hair and tinged with just as much red. He narrowed his blue eyes, and for a moment they looked calculating. Then in a flash that impression was gone. He merely looked a run-of-the-mill man, disappointed in not being able to buy dinner for two women as he wished.

"Then we'll do it another time. You remember that. I owe you both a dinner."

Linda made herself smile. "You don't owe us anything, Mr..." She pretended not to remember his name.

"Roland Barns. Roland, to you."

Linda nodded and tugged on Melanie's arm.

The deputy accompanied them to the car. He leaned against Melanie's window after seeing her into her seat. "I'll drop by when I can. Can't have you two feeling ignored. And just in case those men decide to bother you again, they'll see you're being looked after proper."

Linda started the engine. "You believe us about the men now?"

Roland grinned hugely. "Honey, I believe anything you tell me."

Linda ground the gears into reverse. She didn't reply as she started to back the car into the street, causing the deputy to hurriedly straighten.

MELANIE WAS SILENT as they left the town. Linda twitched in her seat. She didn't like the man. She didn't know why; he had given her no particular cause except for not believing them at first. But she didn't like him. She glanced at Melanie, wondering if once again she was going to make some kind of comment about her behavior.

"Well?" Linda said at last. "Aren't you going to tell me how rude I was?"

Melanie looked across at her. "About what?"

"About that man."

Melanie smiled teasingly. "I think he likes you."

"I don't like him."

"I could never tell."

"Anyway, maybe it's you he likes," Linda responded, deciding to tease back.

"Oh, no!"

"Maybe."

"No," Melanie denied, shaking her head. "I hope not. Because I don't like him either."

The two sisters' gazes met and they giggled. Then the giggles turned into genuine laughter.

Finally Linda asked, "How did he get you into the café?"

"He practically dragged me. I told him I was perfectly all right, but he insisted."

"That's what you get for staying in the car."

"I won't ever do it again...at least, not when he's around."

They laughed again, and Linda's heart swelled. It had been such a long time since the two of them had had anything sisterly to really share or to laugh about. Not since before their father's death...or the accident that had left Melanie almost dead.

Linda's hands tightened on the steering wheel. No. That was the past. It was the future that counted. And for the first time since starting on their crusade, she experienced a moment of genuine optimism. She treasured it.

Chapter Five

Linda concentrated on the task at hand. She held the shallow pan and rotated it counterclockwise, then made a series of short, sideways movements that were supposed to clear away debris and settle the gold into the riffles...if there had been any gold. At the moment she was working with twelve pieces of lead shot that Tate Winslow had dropped into her pan and told her to practice with.

Linda paused to brush away a stray blond hair with the back of her hand. The morning was growing hot. With each successive shovelful of sand and gravel that Tate had dug from the edge of the stream and screened into her pan, her arms were growing tired and her back protested keenly. But she wasn't going to admit to any discomfort. She would sit on a boulder at the edge of the water and work with the cursed bird shot until she recovered each and every one.

The process was slow. She had to wash and rewash the material, first underwater and then out, being careful not to slop anything that she didn't wish to lose over the side of the pan. She had to do it bit by bit, picking out the larger pieces of gravel, smashing any packed material with her fingers and jettisoning only that which she didn't want to keep, all the while being careful not to wash her precious "gold" into the stream. She had progressed from retaining only two lead shots to retaining ten. That wasn't good enough, though. She was determined to keep each and every one. To prove to herself—to prove to *him*—that she could do it.

She glanced over to where he was crouched beside Melanie, helping her with her pan, showing her how to dip it underwater and agitate it at the same time. At first Melanie had been content to watch; then she had wanted to participate.

Linda made a face. She was glad his attention had been drawn away from her; she would much rather work by herself. She was at the point in the process where, as instructed, she turned the pan until the riffles were facing away from her, and gently spread the remaining concentrate along its bottom. It was then that she suddenly focused on something bright floating in the water that remained. She tapped the pan, making the bright particles dance. Then realization dawned, and she could barely contain her excitement. She had found gold. *Gold!*

A triumphant cry burst from her lips as she jumped up from her position by the stream and hurried over to share her discovery.

"I've found some! I've found some!" Linda cried excitedly, looking first at the pan to reconfirm her discovery and then at Tate. "See! It's gold, isn't it?" Linda prompted happily.

He straightened and reached for the pan. Tate placed a finger against the bright bits and they immediately sank. "It's gold, all right."

Linda squealed. She reached for Melanie's hand and squeezed it.

"It's flour gold. That's why it floats."

Some of Linda's excitement abated. "Is that bad?" she questioned.

Tate's dark eyes met hers. "Finding gold is never bad. But this..." He pushed the particles around again. "This is so light, it's hard to recover. Remember, I told you gold is heavier than most everything around it."

"But it's still gold."

"And not fool's gold?" Melanie asked.

Tate shook his head. "No."

"How can you tell?" Melanie persisted.

"If we had a bigger piece I could show you. Fool's gold—pyrite—crushes into powder. Gold doesn't."

"But this is *still* gold." Linda came back to the fact.

Tate nodded.

"Is it worth anything?"

"A lot of it together is."

"But it takes a lot."

"Right. You can pan all day finding this and still have less, by weight, than a piece of gold the size of a grain of rice."

"Rice!" Melanie echoed.

Tate nodded. "Usually in placer mining—that's what you're doing here—it's even smaller."

"And how much of that does it take to make an ounce?" Again Linda wanted to get to facts.

"That depends on the size. A piece the size of a grain of rice could weigh two or three grains—maybe five. A pennyweight of gold is equal to twenty-four grains. It takes twenty pennyweights to equal a troy ounce."

Linda did some fast mental calculations while looking down at her pan. In comparison, her find now seemed as nothing. Her joy turned to disappointment. "So what do I do with this? Toss it back in the water?"

"You can if you want. Though most people count any gold found as valuable."

Chastised, Linda asked, "So what do I...? How do I...?"

"Use a magnet or quicksilver to separate the black sand. Then you put the gold in a bottle and keep it until you get more. Soon you have enough to be worthwhile."

"You make it sound so simple," Linda countered, aggressive because he sounded so maddeningly calm. This was their *life* he was talking about. Their ability to continue to make their way in the world.

He shook his head, smiling slightly. "No one ever said prospecting was easy. If it were, a lot more people would be doing it."

"Just how do you know so much about it? And if you know so much...why aren't you at some claim or other trying to find gold yourself?"

"I did enough of that as a child. My father was a miner."

"And did he strike it rich?" she taunted, wanting to prick at him the way he pricked at her.

His face suddenly lost all expression and when he spoke his voice was clipped. "No."

Melanie forced her way into the conversation. "You say people find these grains of rice?"

For a moment Tate was silent, then at her choice of words, he smiled. "Gold the size of rice grains," he corrected. "Yes, they do."

"In streams like this?" She indicated the water flowing by.

"Definitely in streams like this."

"How do they find them? Panning?"

He nodded. "And by suction dredging."

"Which is quicker?" Linda intervened.

Tate looked at her estimatingly. "Got gold fever pretty bad, don't you?"

"Please answer the question."

Tate didn't hesitate. "Dredging."

"Then why did you waste our time with this?" Linda demanded, shaking the pan at him.

He answered, "Because panning is used in every phase of placer mining. To test a stream, to do the cleanup work after dredging."

"Show me how," she demanded.

"You're not ready for it yet."

"I am. We are." She quickly included her sister in the argument, hoping for an ally. But Melanie remained silent.

"The big thing in looking for gold is patience. A person can't expect to come here, make a killing and leave, all in the space of a few weeks."

"Wouldn't you?" Linda challenged him. "Wouldn't most people?"

"Sure, but they would be wrong. The reality of looking for gold is long-term. If you expect it to be anything else, you might as well pack up and leave right now. There's no use putting yourself through all the trouble."

"We're staying," she said, gritting her teeth.

"Then learn first things first. Get good at what I've shown you." He looked into her pan again and counted the lead shots. He counted twelve. "Good, you got them all." Linda held up her chin proudly. "Now do it again. And again. Get really efficient. Then, and only then, will you be ready for other things."

Linda wanted to continue to argue. She *was* impatient. If there was gold in the river, she wanted to find it. She looked at the flowing water. In some places, where it was shallow, she could see round, well-worn rocks and gravel. Was she looking at some of those grains of gold, hidden beneath the other materials' lighter weight? And nuggets. He hadn't mentioned nuggets. But she knew that they were found in placer streams, too. Her reading had told her that.

Without another word, Linda went back to the spot where she had been working earlier, dumped the remaining concentrate from her pan into a bucket for future separation, and dug into the moistened dirt for another shovelful of gravel. Then she settled down next to the stream and plunged her pan into the cold water.

MELANIE SIGHED as she watched her sister silently stalk away. How often had she seen Linda's straight back set in determination? Sometimes the very energy of her sister's determination exhausted her, especially since the accident. Yet if it hadn't been for Linda, she probably wouldn't be alive right now. Linda had sat beside her hospital bed day and night and willed her back to life. With her determination. With her love. And she had survived, even when she wasn't sure that she wanted to.

A man's face flashed into Melanie's mind. The face of the man she had killed...at the moment before their cars struck head-on. He had looked shocked, surprised...afraid.

Melanie made a soft sound and forced the remembrance away. She had to. Otherwise... Otherwise she couldn't get through a single day. She was alive, while he was dead. Why was she alive? Why was he dead? The questions didn't stop. Not unless she made them.

She spoke to the man at her side. He, too, was staring after Linda's departing form. Her words were conciliatory. "She doesn't meant to be rude. She just..."

Tate Winslow swung around to face her. He smiled slightly. "Some people take to it naturally, I suppose. Don't worry, I'm not offended. I have a fairly tough hide."

Melanie's pale eyes moved over his face. Something she saw there made her doubt the bravado of his words. He was a handsome man, with strong features, but there was a certain vulnerability she sensed deep inside him that conflicted with the aura of control he wore. "Still..." she said softly.

He made a restive movement with one hand. "Don't worry about it. Do you want to keep on with the panning lesson?"

"Do you think I might find some gold like Linda did?"

His smile widened. "It's possible."

"Then let's keep going. I want to learn how to do this. I want to be useful."

Tate squatted at her side as she resumed her position by the stream. He scrutinized the paleness of his pupil's skin. An unhealthy pallor. She looked so delicate, so fragile. Not for the first time did he wonder exactly what she and her sister were doing here, obviously in such a hurry to strike it rich. He probed carefully. "You've been ill?"

Melanie's hands paused in swirling the pan beneath the surface of the water. "You could say that," she answered.

He remained silent, letting her make the decision whether to go on.

Melanie sighed and said, "I was in a car accident."

"Were you badly hurt?"

"Yes."

He glanced at Linda. She was concentrating fiercely on what she was doing. He was sure that she would catch all twelve shot again, just because she was so determined. "And your sister?" he prompted. His gaze remained on Linda, watching as her blond hair gleamed in the golden rays of the sun.

"Sometimes I think she was more hurt by the accident than I was... although she wasn't in the car with me. She had to deal with everything after—" Melanie stopped suddenly.

Tate sensed the intense pain behind her words and he pressed no further. If anyone knew how difficult life could sometimes be, it was him.

He let several seconds pass then said, "No, don't let the lip fall so far." He lifted the edge of the pan a degree, calling her attention back to the process she was learning. "If you do that, you're going to lose everything you have."

His casual words cut at Melanie's soul, slashing into her previous wound. They might lose everything they had...and all because of her. Linda blamed herself, but Melanie knew who the real culprit was. If she hadn't been so careless, there would have been no call on the insurance that turned out to be in arrears...and that man, Albert Johnson, would be alive today.

She took an unsteady breath, again forcing his face from her mind. Her fingers trembled slightly as she continued to swirl the pan beneath the cold water. Tears of weakness blurred her vision. She had no idea if she was working the pan properly.

Once again Tate started to correct her method, but after a quick glance at her expressive face, he remained silent.

A SHORT TIME LATER, possibly no more than ten minutes, Melanie murmured that she had to rest. Tate made no protest. He watched as she walked tiredly to the cluster of trees and sat down, leaning her head back against the sturdiest trunk.

His gaze switched to her sister. Linda looked up, saw her sister's change of position, then saw him looking at her and quickly returned her attention to the stream.

A slow smile tilted Tate's lips. The sisters were so different; he had thought that once before...before he had gotten to know them a little better. Now he knew it was fact. One was sweet and gentle, the other all prickles and aggression. He began to move toward Linda even before he was aware that he was doing so. His arrival was met with silence.

"How're you coming?" he asked, forcing her to acknowledge his presence.

Her pale eyes flashed as she lifted her face. She and her sister looked alike... yet the differences in their personalities strongly marked their features. One was a wounded dove; the other a pugnacious hawk.

"I've gotten them all five times straight. How much longer do I have to do this?" she demanded.

"You're a quick learner."

"I have to be."

Tate let the comment pass. He glanced at his watch. "I have to get back to town to relieve Roland." He wondered at the derisive snort she gave. "So I can't show you anything more today. Think you can wait until tomorrow?"

She brought the pan out of the water and rested it on the gravel at her side. "If I have to, I will."

No thank-you. No pretense of false gratitude. Just a simple, straightforward answer. Tate was becoming more intrigued in the face of her resistance than he might have if she had been more malleable, which surprised him because he had never cared for aggressive women. Miriam was intense, but in a quiet, calm way. Her passion was her career; her fire burned in a controlled atmosphere, never flaring into anything threatening.

All at once Tate felt as if he were plunging into another world, where passion was white-hot and need was uncontrolled. Mentally he jerked himself back, trying to regain his equilibrium. He felt knocked off balance, winded, but his breathing was no different now than it had been a moment before... before he had experienced that wild internal roller coaster ride. A casual observer would have seen no difference in the man as he stood there, seemingly pondering a reply. Certainly Linda Conway hadn't noticed anything unusual.

Tate's first instinct was to get away—from the place, from her. And giving in to that momentary cowardice, he did just that. "Yeah," he said, "I guess you will. Ah—I'll see you tomorrow morning." He glanced at his watch again to give evidence of his hurry, feeling the need to cover his flight and not understanding that, either.

He waved at Melanie as he started toward the board across the stream. She didn't see him... at least she didn't acknowledge his wave, something she would have done if she had. He knew that much about the younger sister. About the older one... all bets were off. He knew nothing. Except that she disturbed him.

MRS. ARMBRUSTER was in the sheriff's office when Tate arrived back in town. And for the first time in their almost nonexistent acquaintance, Tate was glad. Being able to focus annoyance against the woman let him release some of his annoyance with himself for the crazy way he had reacted at the Conway claim. Bertha Armbruster was the perfect target, especially since she was in the process of attacking a man whom Tate respected and cared for.

Passages of Gold 75

He stepped into the office, having been warned of her presence on the sidewalk outside; her haranguing voice carried clearly through the closed door.

Patrick was standing up to her, but Tate could tell that he was wearing down. Patrick looked old, much older than his sixty-two years.

The woman was leaning over his desk, her plump body quivering with rage. "I expect you to *do* something, do you hear? My father wouldn't just leave. Something's happened to him. Like something's happened to the others. And you've done nothing. Nothing! You're little better than an incompetent fool. An old, incompetent fool at that. Why don't you step down like the people of this town want and let someone else take over? Your deputy seems able."

She twisted around when Tate angrily slammed the door. Her enraged eyes met his, and she sniffed before returning to her harangue. "Not *that* one. The other one. I've heard nothing but good said about him. And he has some excellent ideas—"

Tate spoke softly, cutting into the woman's words. "Patrick, would you like me to escort the lady out of the office, or would it be better to escort her out of town?"

Mrs. Armbruster glared at him. "You wouldn't dare," she declared. "I have every right to be here."

"This isn't San Francisco, ma'am. Amador Springs is a tiny place... and we're the only law. You give us trouble, we can put you in jail for disturbing the peace, or for hindering an investigation. That's why I suggested getting you out of harm's way. It seemed the easiest solution."

"What investigation?" she demanded. "And I don't like to be threatened, young man."

"Neither do we," Tate countered. "That's another charge we could look into."

The woman was almost beside herself with anger. "How dare you talk to me like that! Why, I'll... I'll..."

Patrick intervened. "Just have a little more patience, Mrs. Armbruster. That's all we ask...a little more patience."

"No one seems to care about what happened to my father. No one but me!"

"We *all* care," Patrick contradicted her. "It's just slow going sometimes." He took a deep breath and ran a hand through his bushy white hair. His voice was softer when he spoke again. "Now, why don't you do as my deputy says and find some place to relax, and let us get on with what we have to do?" He looked at Tate. "Why don't you take Mrs. Armbruster over to the café and get her a nice hot cup of coffee?"

"I don't want coffee—not from him," the woman said, giving Tate a hard look. "I don't want anything from any of you, except that you do your job!"

"That's what we're trying to do, Mrs. Armbruster," Patrick answered.

The woman sniffed and set her shoulders for her march across the room. At the door she said, "I'm calling my lawyer when I get back to my room. We'll see what he has to say about all of this." Then, as a parting shot directed at Patrick she said, "People *are* talking, you know. Almost everyone here thinks you've outlived your usefulness."

Stiffly, Patrick answered. "They'll have a chance to make themselves heard next election, ma'am."

She sniffed disdainfully once again, then stepped onto the sidewalk, moving like a gunboat filled with missiles ready to be launched.

Patrick dropped back into his seat. "That woman carries a punch," he murmured as he wiped perspiration from his face with a handkerchief he had pulled from his back pocket.

"Maybe her father disappeared because he wanted to get away from her," Tate suggested.

Patrick shrugged, the dawn of a smile on his lips. But he sobered before he made a return comment. "This job is all I have, Tate. I don't—" He swallowed the rest of the tight confession, a man too proud to let himself sound weak.

Tate's gaze was troubled as it swept over his friend. He didn't know what to say. He, too, had heard the rumblings that were growing louder with each passing day. It was as if some outside force was stirring things up... making people restless. Patrick was getting older, yes. But that didn't mean he had become incompetent overnight.

"We just need a little more time," he said in the end, groping for words of assurance.

Patrick lifted his head, his gray eyes holding a weary wisdom. "Time and trouble wait for no man. Well, in my case, I've got loads of one and not enough of the other... and a whole pack of people who think I'm getting too old. I'm beginning to wonder if that isn't so myself." He paused. "I have to ask myself that, don't I?"

The doubt behind Patrick's question wrenched at Tate's heart. Patrick had never questioned himself. His feet were always planted rock-solid on the ground. It had been that quality about him that had allowed Tate to have such confidence in him as a boy...to hold onto him emotionally, while the rest of his life was a maelstrom of indifference, shame and pain.

Now, with this question, it was as if Patrick had become the child and he, Tate, the rocklike strength. A switching of place, a shift of time and responsibility. Tate drew a breath, realizing the importance of Patrick's trust in him. He might not be trained in law enforcement; he might still have conflicts inside himself that might never be resolved. Sometimes he might still feel himself a child, desperately wanting his father's love while at the same time being humiliated by his actions. Loving him, trying to care for him, yet hating him all at the same time, because Dan Winslow never gave any love in return. Still, Tate was the one Patrick had turned to in his time of trouble. He was the one close friend—son—that Patrick relied on.

Tate kept his expression schooled and his voice steady as he answered, "I don't think you should ask yourself anything, Patrick. That's not your style. All the time I've known you, you've never shirked a difficult problem. And I don't think you're about to start now." He paused. "People's opinions swing in the breeze. You know that. One week they're upset about this, the next they're upset about something else. Don't waste your time worrying about them.

"I seem to remember you telling me something like that when I was a boy...when I was upset about my dad and the way people looked at him when they'd find him sprawled on the sidewalk. Well, I'm telling you the same thing now—don't let public opinion get in your way. You've been sheriff here for over forty years. You know your job inside and out. You know the people, you know the place. And no one—no one—can do a better job.''

Patrick gradually unclasped his fists as Tate's words rolled over his bent form. Then his back slowly began to straighten, and he lifted his head as a spark of confidence returned to his eyes.

Patrick cleared his throat and stood up. He gave his pants a positive hitch as he came around his desk to confront Tate.

Tate remained still, knowing from his friend's expression that he had helped him.

Instead of speaking, Patrick reached out to draw Tate into a great bear hug. Then, just as quickly as the physical expression was born, it ended. Patrick was stepping away, clearing his throat again and rehitching his pants.

"Gotta go check something out," he said gruffly, avoiding Tate's eyes.

The heels of the sheriff's boots scuffed the floor in their usual manner as he walked to the doorway. Then he was gone with a slightly self-conscious wave.

Tate stared after him without saying a word. A knot of emotion was in his throat. He couldn't have spoken if forced.

Chapter Six

Linda was out at the stream bright and early the next morning. She had long since given up working with bird shot and was now going after the real thing. Instead of taking shovelsful of sand and gravel from the edge of the stream, she had moved farther into the stream itself, not knowing if what she was doing was right but relying on instinct to guide her. She had started doing that last evening after Tate Winslow left, and had already found a number of tiny granules of gold—larger and heavier than the flour gold she had discovered yesterday, yet not nearly in line with his "grain of rice" size. For the past hour, though, there had been nothing. Pan after pan came up empty of anything valuable.

She glanced at the lean-to, wondering if Melanie was awake yet. When she had slipped out of her bedroll earlier, her sister had been tossing restlessly in a dream. Before leaving, she had smoothed the damp hair away from Melanie's forehead and her sister had calmed. Since by now Melanie was usually awake, Linda decided that she would take a break and see.

But before she finished securing her gear, a visitor appeared near the gnarled oak tree across from her and started down the embankment after calling a hearty hello. The visitor was Roland Barns.

Without being wholly conscious of the furtive movement, Linda hid the tiny glass bottle containing her granules of gold in the pocket of her loosely fitting shirt.

Roland stopped on the other side of the stream. "You look pretty professional doing that," he complimented. "Having any luck?"

Linda didn't return his smile of greeting. She barely returned an answer to his question. "Not really," was all she said.

Roland acted as if he didn't notice her reticence. "It takes a while sometimes. But you look pretty lucky. You'll probably strike gold in no time." He glanced around the camp. "Your sister not here?" he asked, but went on before she could answer. "I'm only askin', because it probably wouldn't be a good idea for either of you to wander too far off. Kinda stay close to your camp."

"Why?" Linda frowned. Tate had said nothing. What was Roland Barns getting at?

At that moment Melanie came out of the lean-to door, rubbing sleep from her eyes, unaware that they had company. She yawned uninhibitedly and stretched her arms, causing the tail of her sleep shirt to rise up her thighs. When she became aware of Roland's presence, she immediately dropped her arms; a wave of embarrassed color stained her cheeks before she fled back into the safety of the shelter.

Roland Barns was grinning widely. Linda didn't like the way he had looked at Melanie. Coming back from town, she had teased her sister that the deputy was interested in her, but she hadn't seriously meant it. Now she wasn't so sure.

She shifted forward, drawing his attention back to her. She could handle him; Melanie couldn't. And she wasn't going to give him an opportunity to try anything with either of them.

"How can I help you this morning, Deputy?"

"Roland. The name's Roland."

Linda waited. When it became apparent that she wasn't going to say anything further, Roland said, "I just wanted to warn you about the rattlesnakes. They're pretty bad around here this time of year. And about the mountain lions. We wouldn't want anything to happen to the two of you. That's why I suggested that you stay close to camp."

"We'll be careful."

"Do you have any kind of weapon with you?"

"Do you mean a gun?"

He smiled. "I don't mean a water pistol."

Linda's irritation was growing. They had enough obstacles to overcome. They didn't need more. As long as they hadn't seen a snake or disturbed a mountain lion, they could have gone on for days, for weeks, without having to feel the need to worry.

Then she relented. He was just doing his job, trying to help them. "Thank you," she said. "We'll be fine. Don't worry about us."

"I don't *worry* ... I'm just concerned. Two young women, all alone—"

Linda's lips tightened; this time he backed off his line of conversation. He motioned to the lean-to. "I also came to see if you and your sister would like to cash in on that dinner I owe you. I could be out here about six and take you into town."

Linda didn't hesitate. "Sorry. We can't. We've already made other arrangements."

Roland Barns frowned. "You mean with someone else?"

At that moment, another figure appeared at the tree and, after a second's pause, started down the embankment toward the stream, his long, lean form a contrast to the other deputy's shorter and stockier frame.

Roland Barns's mouth curled distastefully. "Not with him—"

"Not with him... what?" Tate asked. He had been surprised to find Roland here. He had also been surprised to feel the degree of tension in the air between Linda Conway and the deputy. For a moment, jealousy slashed through him. Then he drew it under control. Now his surprise was directed toward himself. Still, he held himself steady, waiting for a reply.

"Nothing," Roland growled. "Nothing at all." He switched his gaze back to Linda. "Another time then," he said, much more mildly. "And don't forget what I said. There've been enough accidents around here... enough disappearances. I'd hate to think that one day ole Tate and I might have to be out lookin' for you... or for your sister."

On the surface the words seemed ingenuous, without threat. But something about them made goose bumps break out over Linda's body. She shivered slightly in the warm breeze.

Roland turned away. His gaze met Tate's. The two men looked at each other long and hard, before Roland started up the embankment. No words passed between them, but Tate couldn't help feeling that something evil had just passed close by.

Quickly he looked at Linda to gauge her expression, to see if she shared his intuition. But she was no longer gazing in his direction. She had turned to the lean-to and was moving toward it with a quick, ground-covering stride.

"Is he still out there?" Melanie asked from just inside the doorway. She had changed from her night wear to a pair of jeans and a lightweight cotton sweatshirt.

"He's gone. But Tate's shown up."

Melanie's expressed brightened. "Oh, good."

"Oh, good nothing! I wish they'd both leave us alone."

"I thought Tate was going to show us how to use the dredge today."

"I'm sure I could figure it out."

"And take a week doing it? Linda! Unbend! Accept the fact that some people really do want to help us."

Linda's frown remained dark. "He probably wants something too, just like the other one."

Melanie shook her head, denying her sister's words. "No... he's different. He's..."

At her loss for words Linda turned away. She didn't want to hear her sister list the man's assets.

Tate was standing in the middle of their campsite, looking at something a short distance down the wall of the cliff that rose not far from the rear of their shelter. He turned toward them as they approached. "Did you know that you have a lode mine back there?"

Linda asked, "A what?" for both of them.

"A lode mine. A regulation mine. I wonder if your uncle was working it, too."

"Did you know our uncle?" Melanie asked.

Tate shook his head. "I left here a long time ago and only returned the first part of this month. He was gone by the time I arrived."

Something that had been playing in the back of Linda's memory prompted her next question. "Was there anything unusual about the way Uncle Roger died?"

Tate's dark eyes probed hers. "Why do you ask that?"

"Just something someone said." Actually it was the old man at the service station on the day they arrived. He had said something about an accident and then quickly shut up. At the time she had filed it away because of the situation they had been in. Until now. However, she wasn't going to say who her source was. Not when that information had been met with derision once before.

"About your uncle?" Tate prompted.

"About an accident. Forget it. I'm sure it didn't mean anything."

Tate watched her narrowly for another moment before saying, "All I know about your uncle's death is that he had a fall. Someone came out here, found him and brought him into town. He never regained consciousness."

"He fell?"

"Not all that unusual. He was an old man, wasn't he?"

Linda nodded. "In his early seventies...he was our father's oldest brother."

"I can find out who found him, and you can talk with him."

Linda shook her head. She wasn't here to investigate her uncle's death. She really had no cause to wonder about it. He was an old man, and old men sometimes did fall. And if he had been lying out here, exposed to the elements for God knows how long... She continued to shake her head. "No. I'm not concerned about that. I was just asking."

Melanie brought them back to the earlier subject. "Where's the mine?" she asked.

It was a moment before either Linda or Tate looked at her. Each was absorbed in their own thoughts about Roger Conway: Linda, remembering him the last time she had seen him—a happy-go-lucky kind of man, who liked to tease his nieces and drink good beer; and Tate, who wondered if there was more to the story of Roger Conway's demise than had previously been considered. Both looked at Melanie, blinked, then turned to the wall of the cliff.

"Back there—over to the left—it's that dark indentation," Tate explained.

The three of them moved to the spot. As they came closer, the roughly dug indentation in the side of the wall's sheer face could be made out more clearly. It was wide enough for two men to walk inside side by side and a little above the average height of a man. The gloom inside made further visual penetration impossible.

"Do you have a flashlight?" he asked.

Linda ran back to the camp and found one. They had brought one of their own and found several working ones among their uncle's things. She handed it to Tate upon her return.

He took it and disappeared inside. They watched as he flashed the bright beam along the sides of the digging and over the timbers that were meant to stabilize the roof. Soon he came back outside. "Well, that answers that question."

"What?" the sisters prompted, almost together.

Tate smiled. "Your uncle didn't use it. He couldn't have. Those beams are so old they could collapse at any moment. No one should even go in there, much less try to work it."

"Are lode mines more profitable than a stream?" Linda wanted to know.

Tate looked at her. "If you find a vein."

Linda gazed at the opening. She wondered if gold had ever been found there.

"You aren't thinking of—" Tate started to say when Melanie interrupted.

"No! Definitely not. Linda, we're not...right?"

Linda slowly turned. "No. I want to find gold, but I'm not stupid. Anyway, it probably would cost a bundle to get the timbers repaired."

"And there might not be any gold in there," Tate reminded them.

The three started back to the stream. For some reason—bragging? she didn't know—Linda dug into her pocket and brought out the glass vial containing the gold she had found that morning. "But there is gold in the stream. Look!"

Melanie took the vial and gazed at the precious metal inside. Her smile widened.

When the vial was handed to Tate, he shook some of the granules of gold into his palm and looked at them closely, prodding them with his finger.

"It's been a long time," he murmured. For a second the old jubilation was upon him—the fever to possess riches. Even as a child he hadn't been immune. But the craziness soon passed, and he carefully replaced the tiny bits in the vial and returned them to their owner. "You found these panning?"

Linda nodded, and when he smiled she felt ridiculously gratified. She might have been a backward pupil being rewarded for good work.

"You want to learn how to work the suction dredge?" he asked after a moment.

"That's what I'm here for."

IT DIDN'T SURPRISE Linda in the least when Tate once again corrected her. "You're overloading the system. Pull up a bit... wait... now settle it back to the bottom. Sweep the nozzle slowly back and forth. That's it."

For the past hour she had been standing in waders, hip deep in the middle of the chill stream, with the dredge—which had been among her uncle's possessions—floating on two large tire tubes in the water behind her.

Her fingers tightened on the hose as it busily sucked gravel and sand from the bottom of the stream and

Passages of Gold 89

deposited it in the dredge's elongated sluice box. The gasoline-powered engine, located directly behind her, was whining loudly, changing sound as she continued to vacuum—at least as she tried to vacuum. Her spastic handling of the hose was what was drawing Tate Winslow's corrections.

But at least now he was letting her make her mistakes alone. He wasn't standing close beside her as he had been earlier, their hands tangling each time she did something wrong...their bodies bumping together.

As she sucked up more material from the bottom of the stream, she couldn't help but give an occasional glance at the sluice box, curious to see if she had brought up any gold.

"Ready for the next step?" he called after another few moments had passed.

"Yes," Linda replied, yelling over the noise of the engine.

"Work your way over here." He indicated the side of the stream close to where he was standing.

Linda's legs pushed against the water.

Tate reached for the large tub he had brought with them earlier. He wasn't wearing waders; the cold didn't seem to affect him. "Bring it a little closer," he said, motioning to the dredge. "Swing it around and cut the engine."

Linda did as he directed and watched, fascinated, as he placed the tub in the water and let it fill partway so that it would sink to the shallow bottom. He then positioned the narrow end of the sluice box in the tub. "Okay. Now you unlock this." He unlatched a closure. "Then this—then lift the riffle ladder up." He glanced up to see that she was watching. "Now we wash any bits that might be clinging to it into the tub." He dipped water with a small coffee can. "Next we roll up the matting and do the same thing to it." He put his words into action, collecting the burlap material that had rested beneath the riffles. As he slowly began to unfurl it, he carefully washed it with water. He washed the material several times, his patience seemingly inexhaustible. Finally he laid it aside and began to pour water over the sluice box itself, careful that the discharge ran into the tub.

"Think you can do that?" he asked.

Linda gave a short nod.

"Okay... after all that you work the material from the tub the same way you worked the finer gravel you washed by hand from the stream in your pan. You can do it now, or you can do it later if you want to dredge some more."

"I want to dredge more," Linda quickly responded.

Tate looked around for Melanie. A few minutes before she had been watching them; now she was gone.

In answer to his unspoken question Linda explained, "She usually takes a nap about now."

Linda had kept her sister out of the cold water with the excuse that their uncle had left only one pair of waders. Melanie had protested that she would like to learn first, but Linda had pulled rank. After seeing the energy needed to work the operation, Melanie had not pressed to have her turn. She had been content to watch.

Linda primed the pump by herself, remembering her actions of a short time before. Then she started the engine and moved back toward the middle of the stream, toward the boulders Tate had pointed out. He had told her that gold often concentrated at impediments in its journey downstream and that it also liked to travel the quickest path.

This time when she lowered the nozzle to the streambed, things were not quite so chaotic. She still felt awkward, but her determination made her a quick learner.

A half hour later—after going through the entire process once again—she was quite proud. He'd only had to correct her movements once.

Tate stood at the edge of the stream, watching her work. She was small, but she was strong. And she handled the equipment as if born to it. It would be no time before she had the system mastered.

"Very good," he said when she looked at him for comment after she finished.

For the first time Linda smiled, and it totally transformed her face. The mixture of pride and excitement for a job well done brought her to the brink of breathless beauty. It was certainly enough to make him catch *his* breath. Then the smile was gone, replaced by her usual intent aggressivity.

"You've done this a lot, you say?" she questioned.

"When I was a child."

"So what do you think our chances are?"

Tate was slow in answering. "I don't think they're any worse than anyone else's."

Linda straightened. "That doesn't answer my question."

Tate shrugged. "There's no way anyone can guarantee anything. Two people working the same stream—one gets rich, the other dies without making a strike." He paused. "Who knows?"

"But you don't think because we're women we can't do the work."

"If I did, I wouldn't have wasted my time teaching you."

Linda nodded. Ever since her father's death, it seemed as if everyone around them had treated them as incompetents. Of course, she had made a mistake. But who hadn't at one point in time in their lives? One tiny mistake. Then Melanie was involved in the accident.... She stopped that line of thought. She looked at Tate Winslow. Since their arrival, he had treated them fairly. And so far he hadn't asked for anything in return.

"Thank you," she said.

The simplicity of her statement didn't surprise him. The fact that she had said it did.

"I like to be of help." He glanced toward their shelter. "Your sister said she'd been in an accident."

Linda stuffed her hands into her pockets. They were still cold from the water, but mainly it gave her something to do. She nodded.

"She said it was pretty bad," he prompted.

"She was almost killed." Linda didn't want to talk about the accident. Not then. She changed the subject. "Is this all there is to it?" she asked, motioning to the dredge she had pulled onto the bank.

"Isn't this enough?"

Linda glanced at the dredge. It was enough, all right. But she would learn to control the monster, and together they would find gold.

"You could always dive," he murmured.

"Dive?" she echoed.

"In the deeper parts of the stream. But that's a lot more complicated...not to mention dangerous."

"I'm not afraid of danger."

"Just guns," he teased, referring to their first meeting.

"Guns that are pointed at me," she agreed. Then asked, "Did you ever find anyone who'd seen those men?"

He shook his head. "Not a person."

"That's really strange."

"The gold country covers a lot of miles. They could be anywhere in the Mother Lode from Mariposa to Downieville."

Linda was silent, thinking of the men. She wondered if they'd found any gold on her and Melanie's claim.

Tate brought her back from her deliberation. "I heard more than I was supposed to hear earlier."

"What?" she asked, frowning slightly in confusion.

"I heard Roland ask you two to dinner. And I heard your excuse. It *was* an excuse, right?"

Linda hedged. "Well—"

"Then why not make it true? Come to dinner with Patrick and me. It'd sure make a change from out here." When she didn't reply he said, "No strings. Just a nice, quiet meal."

If he had asked purely for himself, Linda would have turned him down immediately. But he had included the older man.

While she deliberated, he said, "Patrick needs a diversion. He needs to take his mind off his troubles, and I can't think of a better way than dinner with two beautiful women." He paused. "And I don't think it would hurt both of you, either."

Linda wanted to refuse. They had come here for one reason and one reason only. But it had been so long since either of them had had a few quiet moments where they could relax, where conversation could flow, and where they could forget about the tragedy that still nipped so closely at their heels.

"All right," she heard herself say. "What time? Where?"

Tate smiled. "Why don't you let me do as Roland proposed—come pick you up about six? That okay? It will be easier that way."

"Easier for who?" she questioned.

"For everyone. You don't know where Patrick lives. I do. I'm staying with him."

Linda frowned. "Are the two of you related?" The two men didn't look anything alike.

Tate laughed. "No."

Her frown increased. "Why do we have to know where he lives? I don't see—"

"It's either dinner at Patrick's, or we eat at the boardinghouse where Roland lives. The café closes at five-thirty."

She said nothing. But she wished now that she had stuck to her original intent.

"A home-cooked meal will do you good," he said. "I'm not so great in the kitchen, but Patrick is."

She moved restively, on the brink of rescinding her agreement.

Tate teased, "If either of us misbehave, you can always call the police."

Linda took his suggestion seriously for a moment before realizing the tongue-in-cheek dryness of his words. A smile was drawn from her. "How reassuring."

"Thought you'd like that." He glanced at the dredge. "Just keep doing what you've been doing. You're coming along pretty fast, but it takes time. If you have any problems, we'll talk about them this evening."

Then he left, telling her once again that he'd be back at six.

Linda stared after him. After all her complaints about him to Melanie, how was she ever going to tell her sister that she had accepted his invitation?

Chapter Seven

Melanie smoothed down her cotton blouse with her hands. "I wish I'd brought along a dress."

Linda looked up from fastening her own blouse. Melanie had been excited about their prospects for the evening. Enough so that Linda wondered if she were developing an attachment for the tall deputy. Either that, or she was secretly starved for social interaction. At the ranch, their lives had not exactly been a social whirl, but they had occasionally had guests. And at those times Melanie had reveled in playing hostess.

"We hadn't planned on anything like this. Jeans will have to do."

"I know, but don't you wish—?"

Melanie kept speaking, but Linda became lost in her own train of thought. She wished a lot of things. She wished that she had never agreed to this evening. She wished that she could again enjoy the give-and-take of simple friendships. At the first sign of trouble most of those old friendships had suddenly dried up. There had been no offers of help from any of the people who could afford to give it.

When she realized her sister was waiting for a reply, she improvised. "You look great in whatever you wear."

Melanie beamed. "So do you."

Linda smiled slowly.

The scrape of a shoe on the gravel outside the door alerted the women to Tate's arrival. Linda glanced at the watch she had slipped on her wrist just for this occasion. Normally she left it on a box by her rolled-up sleeping bag, not wanting to harm it while she worked. He was exactly on time.

THE CAR he led them to was not the open Jeep that Linda expected. This car was long and sleek and kitted out with a rich leather interior. Neither was he dressed as she expected. He was wearing dark slacks and a dark chambray shirt that was open at the neck with a dark cord lacing. With his dark hair and dark eyes, "elegant" was the only descriptive word that popped into her mind.

Melanie must have thought the same, because on the walk up the embankment she squeezed Linda's hand and mouthed an expressive "Wow!"

The drive into town was short and the drive to Patrick McHenry's home even shorter. He lived on the outskirts of Amador Springs in a long, narrow house faced with rock, similar to many built in the past century. It had two stories, and a great oak tree spread its limbs protectively close to the roof.

Tate drew the car to a stop in the driveway and opened the doors for both Linda and Melanie.

"I hope you like spaghetti. That's Patrick's specialty."

They both murmured assent.

Tate smiled and ushered them up the short series of steps onto the porch. The sheriff came out of the kitchen to greet them as they entered the house. He was wearing a large red and white striped apron, which was tied about his round belly and disappeared under his bushy beard.

"Just got things going. Usually I like to let the sauce cook awhile, but this time it's going to have to set up quick." He wiped his hands on the apron and extended one to each of the sisters in turn. "Glad you could make it. Tate tells me you're settling in pretty well."

Melanie smiled shyly, looking about the room that was almost filled with overflowing bookcases.

Linda spoke for both of them. "Yes, we are."

"I won't ask if you've found any gold yet. I've lived around these parts long enough to know better. Sit down...sit down. Tate, why don't you find out what they'd like to drink while I check on things in there?" He motioned to the kitchen with his head.

Tate was smiling slightly as he watched Linda and Melanie react to Patrick's home. He remembered his first visit when he was a boy. He had been almost overwhelmed by the number of books and by the contrast of Patrick's image with his love of learning. The books weren't just for show. Each had been read many times. Neither did they reflect a taste for light reading. Many were histories, both local and world; a number dealt with philosophy and the arts. Patrick's living room had been like the door to the world for him as a child. And Patrick had opened it freely.

"Everything Patrick has is soft," Tate explained, referring to the types of refreshment his friend had to offer. "He doesn't keep alcohol."

"Because of his job?" Melanie asked.

"Because of his convictions."

Each accepted a glass of iced tea. Patrick came back into the room and perched on the arm of a chair opposite to the couch Linda and Melanie were sitting on.

"It's looking pretty good. Won't be long till we eat." He paused, his gray eyes going over the two women. "I don't think I ever extended my condolences about your uncle. He was a fine man."

"Thank you," Linda said, taking a sip from her glass.

"I didn't see him all that often, of course. He kind of kept to himself. But that isn't all that unusual around here."

Tate broke into the conversation. "On the way here, the ladies told me they're from Nevada."

"You don't say. Which part?" Patrick's interest was safely shifted. Tate had succeeded in getting his mind away from the direction it was headed: his troubles.

The sheriff nodded when he was told. "Used to know that part of the state pretty well. I cowboyed there for a couple of years. Of course I was a bit younger then than I am now."

Tate poured a glass of tea and handed it to his friend. He teased, "And here I had always thought that you'd popped into the world in Amador Springs, Patrick."

The sheriff laughed. "Nope...sometimes it just seems as if I've always been here." His face clouded, but before Tate could say anything else to divert him, he said, "Me and that tree outside. Did you notice it when you came in?" He paused for their agreement. "Rumor has it that it used to be a hanging tree—before the house was built. That some of the old Forty-Niners caught a few of their own cheating on food rations. Things sometime got pretty tight for 'em. Anyway, they held a trial and strung 'em up. Rough justice, but I suppose they deserved it."

"Do you ever think about their ghosts and wonder if they might still be around?" Melanie asked.

Patrick shook his great head. "Ma'am, I've got so many other problems to worry about. I think I'd ask one, if I saw it, to come in, just like you, and have dinner with me. We could sit around and talk about old times. I think I'd like to hear what he had to say."

Melanie giggled, Patrick beamed, and Tate and Linda's gazes caught and held. Linda quickly looked away, uncomfortably aware of his tall, dark presence only a short distance away. She squirmed slightly in her seat.

AT THE FINISH of the meal, Patrick pushed back in his chair and said, "Best idea you've had in a long time, Tate." Then, at the front door as he saw them onto the porch, "We'll have to do this again. I can't remember when I've enjoyed myself more. It's sure as hell been a long time, I know that."

Contrary to Linda's presentiment, the dinner had turned out to be enjoyable. Patrick had proved to be a wonderful raconteur. He had kept everyone highly amused with his stories and observations and with his keen sense of humor. As the evening wore on, Linda could see the lines of strain recede from Melanie's features, just as she could see them disappear from Patrick's.

The car started smoothly and drew away, making a half circle in the street to retrace their earlier journey.

Melanie sighed in the back seat, a soft, pleasant sound. "He's nice." She hadn't visibly begun to wilt until shortly before they left. Even now she was still smiling.

"One of the nicest people around," Tate agreed.

"I wasn't sure about him when we first met," Melanie said.

"Neither was I," Tate returned.

Linda glanced at him. That was a curious thing for him to say. But he said no more and she didn't press him. Neither did Melanie. And soon, from the gentle rise and fall of her breast, Linda knew that her sister had fallen asleep.

It was then she suddenly felt claustrophobic. Night had fallen during the intervening hours, and the car might have been a warm cocoon, protecting her from her life's more troublesome worries. Yet conversely it also presented her with a larger concern.

Tate glanced at her and smiled. His smile didn't help. Linda swung her head around to gaze out the window—to pretend to be absorbed in the night, when in truth she was wholly aware of her companion less than two feet away.

The drive back to the claim was silent. He didn't try to break into her thoughts, and she by strong will, might have been alone.

The car stopped in the clearing and Linda immediately stepped out. She was opening Melanie's door, preparing to wake her, when Tate caught hold of her wrist. His eyes glittered strangely as he looked down at her, the starlight seemingly magnified a million times in his dark gaze.

Linda swallowed tightly. She didn't comprehend what was happening to her. She felt lost, alone... but along with those emotions, deeply excited. Her breathing was shallow, as if she were winded after running a race.

"Let me," he said, his voice low and slightly husky.

Linda felt frozen in place. Then she understood and stepped out of the way. He leaned into the car and collected Melanie in his arms.

Linda stiffly led the way to the camp. He followed, cradling her sister's body with great care.

They passed the tree and moved down the embankment to cross the stream. With jerky movements, Linda opened the door to the lean-to. She tried to tell herself that goose bumps had broken out along her skin because she was reacting to the cold. With the loss of the sun, the nights were quite cool. But she knew that wasn't true.

Tate pushed inside, ducking slightly as he entered the room. "Which one?" he asked, looking from one rolled-up sleeping bag to the other.

Linda hurried to spread Melanie's bedding on the floor. She didn't answer, just letting her work speak for itself. She again stepped back when Tate leaned over, finally kneeling to deposit Melanie's limp form on the bedding. Melanie murmured something unintelligible. After gently covering her, he straightened.

Linda nervously rubbed her palms along her jeans.

Tate gave her a long look, then motioned with his head toward the door. Linda stiffly complied. He followed, pausing to close the door carefully behind them.

As she moved outside, Linda's legs felt odd, as if they were made of wood. They didn't want to move properly. She didn't know why she had come out here. She should have refused. She should have—

He came up behind her. She jumped when he placed both hands on her shoulders and turned her to face him.

She tried to look anywhere but into his eyes. "Thanks for the evening," she babbled. "It was really good for Melanie. I think she—"

Her words were cut off by his lips.

Linda gave a tiny gasp. Then the world started to spin. His mouth was warm, probing...and a flood of immediate response rushed through her. For a moment she couldn't think at all; all she could do was feel.

His long body was bent over her smaller one; his arms had come around her back, crushing her to him, lifting her even as one of his hands tangled in her hair.

Then the tenor of the kiss changed to one of savoring. Finally, even that was broken.

Linda was breathless as he straightened. She stared up into his darkly handsome face. She couldn't believe what had just happened. She wasn't even sure if she *liked* the man.

As he continued to look down at her, Linda could have drowned in the blackness of his eyes.

"You can't say you haven't felt that coming on tonight," he murmured.

He still had not released her completely. Both of his hands were branding the skin over her ribs through the thin material of her blouse. Part of her wanted to push away; another part of her very much wanted to stay where she was... wanted him to stop talking and kiss her as he had before.

"I don't know what you're talking about," she managed to say unsteadily.

He smiled. It was as if he knew everything that she was thinking.

Linda forced her release by twisting away. "I don't like to be taken advantage of," she said shortly, attempting to save face. She had to convince him—convince herself—that she hadn't responded so readily. But the feel of his lips still tingled on her mouth, and the tumult of her emotions still ran riot through her body.

Tate had been as surprised by his action as she. It hadn't been planned. More than once during the evening, he had almost been overwhelmed by the desire to kiss her. He had watched the way her mouth moved when she talked, when she smiled, when she was pensive. And he had seen the way she looked at him—long, questioning, almost mesmerizing. But if she was determined to deny it, God knew he didn't need to complicate his life any further. He drew away. "Then maybe we both should forget it."

"Yes," she said, braving things out. "I think that would be an excellent idea."

The dark eyes pierced with starlight watched her for another long moment before he turned to walk away.

Linda stood by the stream, her hands unconsciously curled into fists at her sides. When he could no longer be seen in the darkness, and when the purr of his car's engine ignited, then grew progressively quieter, she drew a halting breath and went to sit on a nearby boulder, the gurgling stream her only companion.

An owl called in the distance. Farther away, his mate answered.

Linda drew a trembling hand through her hair. She gazed at the darkened trees, at the rough walls of rock that made up the little canyon. How many people through time had been in this place? Sitting at night in the quiet like her, wondering where fate was going to take them. Awed by the complexity of life. Hungering for release. Feeling so small beneath the canopy of the heavens, so vulnerable to the forces of nature and of mankind... and so vulnerable to their own weakness of will.

There were times when she wanted to flee, to get away from the problems that confronted her, which she knew was only human. At those times she severely castigated herself. She couldn't leave Melanie, couldn't turn her back on the generations who had gone before her.

But at weak moments, moments like this, she desperately wanted what life had so far denied her.

She touched her lips, reliving an echo of sensation.

From the first second she had seen him that evening, he had been like a dark force, dressed in black, with that thick dark hair and dark, almost fathomless eyes. More than once during the following hours she had looked up to catch him looking at her.

He had been right. She should have expected what had happened. Maybe she had. She could have stayed inside the lean-to. She could have seen him off at the door, closing out temptation, closing away any further chance of turmoil.

But she had done nothing of the sort. When he invited her outside, she had done his bidding. And when he kissed her... it hadn't been her who had broken them apart.

Linda gave a soft, low groan, tears slowly welling up in her eyes. A tear escaped to roll over her cheek unheeded.

Her soul, unable to rest before, was now even less prepared to find respite.

TATE PASSED the turn that would lead him back to Patrick's house. He didn't want to go back there yet. He didn't want to have to talk to anyone, not even his old friend. And Patrick would have waited up, like an old biddy hen, watching out for his charge. Responsibility in Patrick did not die. Not even when the charge he was concerned with was well into his thirties.

His hands tightened on the steering wheel. Maybe he did still need someone to watch out for him, to keep him away from the bramble bushes... to put blinders on him, if necessary.

He was here to help Patrick, not complicate his life with a love affair, even if the lady was willing, which she didn't seem to be. At least, not when she had a bit of time to think about it.

Tate moved in his seat, needing some form of activity besides driving. He pulled the car to a stop and stepped out into the coolness of the night. The moon was late in rising. It was just now peeking over the mountains in the distance. For a moment Tate was completely still, standing like an ancient savage in a mysterious ritual of worship.

The thought caught his fancy. *Him, a savage.* A man who carefully sought to control each aspect of his life...who programmed each day and each night with the intensity of someone who had witnessed too much turmoil. Even his sex life was managed. Once every couple of weeks he and Miriam would get together and satisfy the needs of each other's bodies. Nothing flamboyant, nothing with too deep a meaning. The rest of the time they acted as friends, propping each other up when things went wrong, congratulating each other when things happened to go right.

Miriam was safe. She didn't ask any more of him than he was prepared to deliver. And he didn't ask any more of her. She was no obsession. She was just there, as he was for her. He didn't fool himself that she felt any differently.

She had been mildly upset that he'd been unable to accompany her to Greece this summer. But she hadn't canceled her plans. And he could honestly say that this was the first time he had thought deeply of her since his arrival.

Obsessions...to women...to drink. He had resisted both, just as religiously as his father had not. First one, then the other had ruled his father's life. Somewhere along the line Tate had made the decision not to follow. The very absence of an obsession had become almost an obsession with him. He allowed himself to drink—one drink per occasion, no more. And he allowed himself one woman...a woman who didn't threaten his equilibrium.

Now, with one foolhardy action, he had shattered his hard-won equilibrium all to hell, and he knew he was going to have a devil of a time getting it back in order.

Tate found a low-hung branch of a stunted pine and reached out to it for support, leaning his body against his upraised arms. In the distance he could hear a stream...the same one that flowed by the Conway claim.

In spite of himself, he wondered if she was still awake.

Tate grunted and shook his head, trying to destroy the image and the sensations that rushed to torment him.

He had to admit that she was pretty...too pretty. And he had to admit that he liked the fierceness of her determination. But his problem had surfaced because there was something more, something he could scarcely comprehend...something he shied away from even trying to comprehend.

He straightened. This had to stop. He was acting like a moonstruck boy barely into his teens. Next thing he knew, he would be dreaming about her.

Tate made a motion of disgust and bent down for a rock, which he then tossed with some force into the nearby brush. His action had immediate results. Something small and furry was startled from its hiding place, rushing through the undergrowth as if pursued. Then, not realizing the danger, the mouse broke into the open, running almost directly toward him, its fright causing it to make a terrible mistake.

Tate remained perfectly still. The poor little creature had been disturbed enough. He waited for it to regain cover. Then he moved back to the car, restarted the engine and slid the gears into position, ready to escape himself.

Only for him there was no cover yielding escape... merely more exposure. An exposure he knew he was ill-prepared to deal with.

As LINDA PREPARED their breakfast, Melanie chattered to her about the evening before. "He really is a surprising man. When we first came here, I wasn't sure if I liked him or not. He didn't seem very sympathetic. But Patrick's so nice. And he can tell such great stories!"

Linda made a noncommittal sound. Upon awakening, her thoughts had automatically centered on Tate... because she didn't want them to? Because she had spent most of last night tossing restlessly on the bedroll, trying not to think of him... and yet still thinking of him?

Now Melanie couldn't seem to keep quiet. Her head plainly didn't ache, her emotions didn't feel scattered.

Linda immediately hushed that line of complaint. Her sister had had her share of adversity. If she was happy today, it was the least she could do to listen. Melanie deserved some joy in life. But each time she spoke, particularly about Tate—singing his praises, repeating something he'd said—it was like scraping a fingernail down an exposed nerve.

It seemed to please her that he had carried her from the car to their shelter. "See," she said. "He's not nearly as bad as *you* thought." She paused, frowning slightly. "I think he's had a hard time in his life.

There's something behind the way he smiles... and sometimes it's in his eyes... a kind of sadness."

Linda put a hand to her forehead. She didn't know how much more of this she would be able to take.

Melanie finally noticed her distraction and immediately voiced concern. "Linda? Is something wrong?"

The waver of unease in her sister's voice forced Linda to offer reassurance. She was all Melanie had left. Melanie wasn't strong enough to carry on on her own yet.

"It's nothing. Just a headache." She smiled weakly. "I must have drunk too much coffee last night. I couldn't get to sleep."

Melanie giggled softly. "I can't say I had the same problem."

Linda smiled. "No, you were out like a light."

Melanie's smile faltered. "You didn't have a fight with him, did you?"

"Who?" Linda played for time.

"Tate. Who else?"

Linda slid the egg she was cooking onto a tin camping plate. "Here's your egg. Eat it while it's hot."

Melanie stood her ground. "Did you? Oh, say you didn't. Not after he was so nice to us."

The matter seemed unnaturally important to Melanie. Linda wondered again if her sister was starting to feel more for the man than she would like her to. But then if *she* could, why couldn't Melanie?

Linda shook her head. "No," she lied, "it's just a headache. He—he only stayed for a few minutes after he carried you inside."

"I've seen you pick a fight in much less than that time."

Linda took a deep breath. "We didn't have a fight, okay? I've never pretended to like him particularly. Don't hope for more."

Melanie prodded her egg with her fork. If she ate a portion of it, Linda would feel lucky. One of the things Linda worried about was her sister's lack of appetite.

"You can try, can't you?" Melanie asked at last. Her eyes were large and serious as she raised them to her older sister, who was not proof against her plea.

Linda nodded. "Sure. Sure, I suppose." She slipped the next egg onto her own plate and sat down. After that whopper of a fib, she didn't feel much like eating, either. But the morning's activities were going to be long and hard. She needed a good breakfast behind her.

And anyway, she would do anything to make her sister happy. Wouldn't she?

Chapter Eight

"What's the matter? Did you lose something?" Melanie asked curiously as she came up beside her sister.

Linda was searching through the pile of equipment she had neatly stored beside the cabin the evening before. She couldn't have misplaced her gold pan. She couldn't. But she didn't want to believe that anything else had happened to it. "As a matter of fact, yes," Linda said, straightening.

"What?" Melanie asked.

Linda jammed her hands into her pockets. In the week since the dinner at Patrick's, she had kept the fact of the growing number of missing items from Melanie, other than asking her once if she had seen one of the trowels. She hadn't wanted to worry her. She could withhold the information no longer. "Well, several things actually. It's almost as if a pack rat was at work...only he hasn't left behind anything shiny that I can tell."

Melanie frowned. "What are you talking about?"

Linda sighed. "We've had several things just... disappear: a shovel, two trowels, the tweezers, now my gold pan."

"Are you sure you haven't just misplaced them?"

"That's what I wondered about you."

"Why didn't you ask?"

"I did, remember?"

Melanie nodded slowly, recalling the earlier question. She looked down at the pile again. "Are you sure?"

"I've been through everything three times, and that's just today. No, it's got to be something else."

Melanie shifted position. Over the past few days she had begun to look better. Working in the early-morning sun as well as in the late evening had brought a light tan to her skin. She didn't lapse into dark silences as often. She might be silent—it was her nature not to talk for long periods of time—but at least she didn't seem to be living in the past as often. Intent upon helping wash the concentrate, she had found numerous granules of gold, which had lifted her spirits considerably. "Like what?" she asked.

"I don't know. I wish I did, but I don't."

"Do you think someone's stealing them?" Melanie jumped to the same conclusion as her sister.

"Who? Who's out here to steal anything? We haven't seen a soul since we came here except—"

"And that was days ago. Do you think it *could* be an animal?"

Linda shrugged. A shovel, a trowel and a gold pan were a little large for a pack rat to drag off. The tweezers? Maybe. No, if it was an animal, it was of the two-legged variety. Only why would anyone want to steal anything so innocuous? She didn't understand.

When she was slow to answer, Melanie said, "Maybe we should keep watch tonight, to see what's coming into camp."

Linda agreed, although she wondered what they'd do if her suspicions proved to be correct.

THE MOMENT Tate entered the tiny café, most of the conversation stopped. One person who didn't see him continued speaking. "Patrick just isn't the same as he used to be. That's all. He's gettin' old like me. But then I don't make any claims to—" Someone elbowed him in the side, motioning toward Tate. The man instantly shut up.

His face tight, Tate drank the coffee he obstinately ordered. The taste was extremely bitter. This wasn't the first time he had overheard complaints about Patrick. Gossip was mushrooming in all corners, but there was nothing he could do about it. If he tried to defend Patrick, it would only make things worse for his friend. The people wouldn't listen to him. Not to Dan Winslow's son.

As he left the café, Tate nearly collided with the woman he knew was responsible for much of the gossip. Bertha Armbruster was striding along the sidewalk as if she owned it.

"Look where you're going," she snapped, coming to an abrupt halt to glare at him.

Tate had successfully avoided the collision by hastily withdrawing into the doorway. He now forced his body to relax. "Excuse me," he said with icy politeness. He repeated his step onto the sidewalk.

Bertha Armbruster snorted. "I came here two weeks ago today. I'm no further along now than I was then, and all you can say is 'Excuse me'?" She glanced at the café behind him. "Is that all you people do all day: eat?"

"I was having coffee, Mrs. Armbruster."

"That too. Eat, drink coffee...no one seems to want to stir themselves to *do* anything."

"Everything is being done that can be." How many times had she been told that?

She looked Tate up and down in one quick, not too complimentary gesture. "By you?" she snorted. "I've heard all there is to hear about you. About the way your father drank himself to death. About the way you caused nothing but trouble. Why, it's like having the blind lead the blind!"

Tate stiffened the instant she mentioned his father. "That was a long time ago and absolutely none of your business."

"When it concerns my father, it's my business. And you're not even a proper deputy. You're a teacher at some kind of private school! Probably a reformatory!"

"I'm a professor at a college." Tate was proud of what he had accomplished, even if he wasn't proud of certain aspects of his youth.

"A soft job," she scoffed.

Tate gave a short nod and said, "Think whatever you want to, ma'am." Then he started to move away. If he didn't, he *would* be held responsible for his actions. Friend or no, Patrick would come after him.

Still seething with venom, the woman called, "Why don't you go back to where you came from, and take that worthless old man with you?"

It was a good thing Tate was accustomed to exerting self-control. The habit came in handy at that moment. As it was, he moved stiffly across the street to eventually turn into the sheriff's office.

Patrick wasn't there. He had gone into Sacramento for the morning, planning to meet with a friend attached to the state Department of Justice. Discussing the disappearances, Tate had no doubt.

Roland looked up when he entered the office. Already angry, Tate barely acknowledged him.

Slowly Roland swung his feet to the floor from their position on top of Patrick's desk. "Something drop down out of the sky and sting you?" he asked.

His voice had a needling quality that grated on Tate's nerves. "Just your friend Mrs. Armbruster."

Tate walked to the desk he used whenever Patrick was away. In reality it was Roland's desk, which he kept tightly locked. When Patrick was absent, Roland usurped the larger desk. A psychological game of wishful thinking?

Roland grinned. "She's not *my* friend."

"Then how come she's always extolling your virtues?"

"Can I help it if the woman has good taste?"

Tate stared intently across the distance separating them. "How much of what you say and do is an act, Roland?"

Roland's face went blank, then his usual grin fixed itself firmly back in place. "I don't have any idea what you're talking about."

Tate sat down. He leaned back and entwined his fingers behind his head. "Just that you're really hard to read. You seem to like Patrick. Yet..."

"Yet what?"

"Yet I'm not so sure."

Roland looked heavenward. "Oh, Lord. Now he's trying to use all his book learnin' on me. Why don't you go back to where you're at home, Tate? Leave the police work to the people who can handle it?"

"That's almost exactly what Mrs. Armbruster said."

"You're starting to hallucinate."

"By no stretch of the imagination can Mrs. Armbruster be mistaken for an illusion."

Roland got up, stretched and belched. "There's a saying: if you can't handle the smoke, don't get too close to the fire. Ever hear of it?"

Tate made no motion to answer.

"Well, I'd start watching out for smoke, if I was you, Tate. But then I'm not you. I'm just a plain, simple country boy who never wanted to be anything more."

Again Tate made no answer, and Roland, after giving him a lazy glance, told him that he was going after coffee and would be back later.

Tate's mouth was tightly clamped and his body was again taut. He didn't like Roland Barns and didn't trust him, and despite all the protestations of simplicity, he instinctively felt that there was much more to the man than easily met the eye.

"How LONG do you think it will take?" Melanie's voice broke through the darkness of the shelter.

"It could take all night," Linda answered.

"That long?"

Linda nodded, then realizing she couldn't be seen said, "Yes."

"How're we going to stay awake?"

"*We*'re not. I'm going to stay awake while you sleep."

There was a rustle of protest. "No, that's not fair. I'm getting stronger, Linda. You've got to have noticed. I can pull my weight now."

Linda's heart gave a tiny flip. *If only.* Melanie was looking stronger, that was true. But how long would that last if she was helping during the day and then awake all night, as well?

Unseen, Linda lightly chewed her bottom lip. She had to maintain a delicate balance. She didn't want to discourage Melanie's recovery, but she also didn't want to crush her spirit. She struck a compromise. "What if I take first watch? You get some sleep, and I'll call you later...then I'll get some rest."

"Sounds wonderful!" Melanie's voice lilted. "And you won't forget to call me, right?"

Linda responded to the sudden suspicion behind her sister's words. "I promise. I'll call you."

Melanie gave a tiny, satisfied sigh. Then Linda heard her settle into her bedroll, and soon the sound of soft breathing came to her ears. Melanie was already asleep.

Linda positioned herself against a table leg and yawned. She was almost as tired as Melanie. She had put in long hours the last few days, working the dredge, washing more of the concentrate...and they had realized very little. A few rice-sized grains of gold, a bit more of the fine granules, but not enough to really count.

Linda adjusted her position, easing her spine away from a sharp edge. This was going to be a very long night. She would keep her promise to Melanie, but she was going to take most of the hours herself.

The minutes passed slowly, and her mind jumped from one image to another, the unlighted flashlight, held in readiness, growing heavy until she set it on the floor at her side.

A picture of her father came into her thoughts. He hadn't been a big man, at least not in the physical sense. Neither had their mother been large, which accounted for both her own and Melanie's small build. But Amos Conway had had a forceful personality. He, too, had experienced difficulty with the land he inherited. Several consecutive years of drought had just about wiped him out, but he had survived it. Through intelligent choices, hard work and a will of steel he had hung on, eventually turning the ranch into a healthy financial asset. By the time she was born, and certainly by the time Melanie came along, their parents had been through the test of fire and come out stronger for it.

Linda smiled softly to herself in the dark. Her father had wanted a son, especially a first-born son. He had always tried to hide it, but she knew. And she had tried to fill that position as best she could. She wanted him to be proud of her, to feel that he hadn't been shortchanged. So from early childhood she had gone out with him on ranch chores, doing the same things he did...learning from him. She had gained his approval, although he had been quick to tell her that he loved her for what she was: a caring, enthusiastic, energetic, loyal young woman.

Then one day, after riding out alone to check a suspected break in a fence, he was gone. He'd had a heart attack about five miles from their house, and no one had been there to help him.

Both she and Melanie had been devastated. The ache still pulsed in their hearts. She didn't think the pain of his loss would ever go away completely.

Linda sighed, seeing her father as she had seen him so many times, sitting comfortably in the saddle, grinning crookedly about something, the leathery tan of his rugged face partially shaded by a worn black hat.

Her father... She wished he was there right now, to take her into his arms, to tell her that everything would work out all right. She had always felt so safe when near him. Now she didn't feel safe at all. But she had to pretend for Melanie's sake.

She glanced toward the unseen form on the nearby sleeping bag. Her sister's breathing was slow and even. *The remaining Conways.* There were only the two of them left in the world. The two of them against a society of people to be dealt with, like the insurance company representative who had apologized but said there was nothing she could do, since they had failed to pay the premium. No matter the circumstances, no matter the years of prompt payments...

Linda rested her head against the table leg and closed her eyes. Somehow it felt better in the dark. She tried to empty her mind of all thoughts. All she was doing was hurting herself by remembering.

LINDA STARTED AWAKE. Had she heard something? For a moment she remained perfectly still, but the only sound she heard was the pounding of her heart.

She collected the flashlight at her side and moved stiffly to the door, where she put her ear to the wood to listen. When again she heard nothing, she flicked the flashlight on and off, wanting to double-check that it still worked. She didn't leave it on, though, because she didn't want to showcase her presence when she stepped outside. If someone *was* there, she wanted to have the same advantage of night cover as he, or she, or it. Butterflies fluttered in her stomach. She gritted her teeth, then opened the door and silently slipped outside.

The moon was low in the western sky and didn't do much to illuminate the planet below. Most of what light remained came from the stars; and for some reason, tonight even they seemed less capable of the job.

Linda flattened her body against the side of the shelter, her eyes probing the campsite, looking for movement, watching for anything that might be out of the ordinary.

Her breath seemed cut from her lungs. She had to force herself to breathe at all.

Slowly she eased away from the wall. So far she could see no one. She took several tentative steps, stopped, listened, then took several more, highly conscious of everything around her.

Finally she directed the flashlight around the site. There was nothing. The noise must have been imagined. Then the glowing swath pierced the darkness beside the stream at the point where she had pulled the dredge out after her day's work.

Linda frowned. Something about the dredge's outline wasn't right. She moved closer, still conscious of her exposure, the beam of light guiding her way.

Then she stopped. The dredge was lying flat on the ground, the tubes on either end a shredded mass. She drew a quick breath, the sound mirroring her surprise. Someone *had* been here! Someone who had...

Her hand was trembling as she arced the beam of light across the stream toward the embankment, then back toward the cliff at the lean-to's rear. It might have been a lightning flash, so swiftly did it move.

"Who is it?" she charged hoarsely. "Who's done this? Where are you? Why don't you come out and—?"

Her words stopped. *Come out and what?* Whoever had done this wasn't playing around. This wasn't a prank; this was vicious. And next time they might not stop at slashing old rubber.

Linda hurried back to the shelter, thrusting open the door and throwing herself inside. Her chest was heaving as she fitted the bar across the door and leaned back against it.

A movement in the room caused her to whirl around and shine the flash. Her hand felt frozen to the cylindrical surface. She couldn't have dropped it if she'd tried.

The bright light caught Melanie in the act of sitting up, her eyes large with surprise, her blond hair disheveled.

Linda made another sound, something between a sob and a laugh. It was Melanie. *Dear, sweet Melanie.*

"Linda?" came her sister's questioning appeal.

The light wavered, then fell. Linda fought hard against the hysteria rising in her throat. She swallowed and took several deep breaths.

"Linda...that is you, isn't it?" Melanie had struggled to her feet, poised for flight if the answer proved to be unwanted.

Linda gained control. "Yes, it's...it's me."

"What is it? What's happened? Why are you standing there with the flashlight in your hand? Have you been outside?"

Linda forced herself to move. She went to the lantern and lighted it, adjusting the wick so that the room was bathed in a soft glow.

She felt Melanie's eyes worriedly search her face. "I heard something. A noise. Actually I had fallen asleep and I guess the noise woke me up."

"What was it?"

Linda smiled tightly. "It certainly wasn't a pack rat."

Melanie came toward her, concern written on her face. "What was it?" she repeated.

Linda lifted her gaze and said quietly, "Someone doesn't like the fact that we're here. Either that, or they like to play silly games."

"Are you going to tell me?" Melanie demanded impatiently.

"The tubes on the dredge have been slashed."

Melanie blinked. "Are you sure?"

"It's a little hard to mistake. The dredge is sitting flat on the ground and the tubes are shredded."

"Who'd want to do that?" Melanie cried, the shadows that had started to lift from her eyes rushing back.

Linda cursed the unknown person responsible. She shrugged. "Your guess is as good as mine."

"Do you think it's those men?"

"Trying to drive us away again, you mean?"

Melanie nodded.

Linda hesitated. "It's possible, I suppose. Anything's possible."

"What are we going to do?"

The reemergence of fear in her sister's voice caused Linda's reply to be more bracing than it might otherwise have been. She was just as afraid as Melanie, but she couldn't afford to show it. "We're going to sit right here, of course. We will not be driven from this claim. It's ours, and we're working it."

"But what if . . . ?"

"Sneaking around in the middle of the night doesn't take much courage. Neither does slashing old inner tubes. They're probably just trying to scare us."

"Is it working?" Melanie whispered.

Linda smiled at her sister's decision to frame her fear in the form of a question. "It's working," she conceded. "But we're Conways, remember? It's going to take more than that to really shake us up. Anyway, we need the money."

Melanie looked away, her lips trembling almost imperceptibly. But Linda saw them, and she silently added to the earlier curse she had directed at the person responsible.

UNABLE TO SLEEP, the two sisters talked softly back and forth for the remainder of the night, just as they had when they were children and shared the same room.

"No, I don't think we should," Linda said staunchly to her sister's suggestion that they tell the sheriff or Tate. "It's our business, and we'll handle it on our own. Anyway, it might not happen again. Whoever did this might get discouraged when they see that we're not going to budge. Maybe then they'll leave us alone."

The words sounded good, and Melanie seemed appreciative of their assertion—whether or not she actually believed them. Linda certainly didn't. At least her doubt level was high.

Just before morning dawned, the sisters finally fell back to sleep. Midmorning, Linda awakened and got up as quietly as she could. She went outside to inspect the damage in the day... to see if she had missed the destruction of anything else. She walked slowly to the stream and stopped beside the dredge. It looked even more pathetic in better light. The tubes weren't just cut. As she had told Melanie, they were shredded. Numerous ugly slits marred the rubber.

Linda squatted down to inspect the engine. The gas cap was partially free but not completely loose. Had her appearance startled the person away before he could perform more mischief?

Linda had just begun a survey of the rest of the area, when a voice hailed her from across the stream. She turned. Tate Winslow was standing beside the gnarled tree, looking across at her.

He was smiling slightly.

"What are *you* doing here?" she challenged him, her expression instantly darkening. He was the last person she wanted to see at that moment. She didn't need the complication of his disturbing presence or his office.

He shifted slightly, one hand coming out to rest lightly on the tree's trunk. "Coming to see if you're still alive, I guess. Is that a crime?"

Tate's eyes moved slowly over her. He didn't understand why she had such a power over him, why he felt so drawn to her. He had resisted; he had stayed away a week. Then this morning, after driving out to check a call, he had given in to the dictate of his subconscious and ended up here.

"Well, as you can see, I'm fine," she said. "You've done your duty, now go."

Tate's smile held in place. "Why is it everyone is so ready to see me leave?"

Linda didn't understand what he was referring to, but she said, "Maybe it's your charm."

"So you admit I have some charm?"

Linda gave an exasperated sigh. "I said nothing of the sort. I just meant..."

She stopped when she saw him stiffen. His gaze had gone to the dredge, and she knew that he had seen what had happened to it.

"My God!" he murmured and started down the embankment to step lightly onto the board that crossed the stream. Before she was completely ready, he was squatting beside the dredge, one long finger running along the surface of a slashed tube. "What the hell happened here?" His dark eyes turned up to her, narrowed, intent.

Linda flirted with the idea of denial, but in the end she decided against it. The evidence was apparent. She would only look more of a fool. "I found it like that last night."

He stood, slowly unwinding his frame to its full height. "Someone came here last night? Did you see them?"

"No."

"So how—?"

"I thought I heard a noise and came outside. This is what I found."

He leaned down and jiggled the gas tank lid. It fell off into his hand. He peered inside. "Looks clear, but we'd better check it out before you try to start the engine. Someone could have put sand or something inside to foul it."

Linda closed her eyes in momentary helplessness. Then she ran a hand through her hair, dug her boot heels into the ground—figuratively rather than actually—and said, "I'll take care of it."

His dark eyes remained steadily on her. After a moment they flashed quickly around the surrounding area. "Anything else harmed?"

"Not that I know of."

"Melanie?"

"She's still asleep."

"Does she know?"

"Yes."

Linda wanted him to leave. Her abbreviated answers were ample proof.

He sighed and returned his gaze to her. "You may not think that this is any of my business, but it is. You sure you didn't see anyone?"

"No one."

Tate frowned. He didn't like the look of this. He didn't like it at all. He wished he hadn't touched the gas tank lid, but he hadn't been thinking. Police procedures were not instinctive with him. "Do you have any idea who it might have been?" he asked.

Linda answered his question with a question. "Do you?"

"I think I could come up with an idea or two."

She knew his thoughts had gone in the same direction as hers had earlier.

But their ideas totally disconnected when he continued. "Why don't you and Melanie come into town, get a room at the boardinghouse and let things settle for a few days? Patrick can look for prints on this, send them off and..."

Before he finished speaking, Linda was shaking her head. She hadn't even heard his last suggestion, just the first. "No. No way."

"It would be safer."

Linda shook her head again.

"If it's money you need—" he began.

"Look! I didn't ask you to come here. I didn't ask for your help. You just showed up!" she exploded.

"You wouldn't have reported this, would you?"

Linda lifted her chin. "No."

"Why? Because of the other night?"

Linda felt her cheeks flush. "The other night has nothing to do with this."

"Don't be stubborn. If you won't think of safety for yourself, think of it for Melanie."

"Melanie's just fine as she is."

"What if they come back with a gun again next time?"

"It may not have been them."

"Who else would do this?"

"We will not be run off our claim!"

"Gold means that much to you?"

Linda refused to answer.

Tate couldn't take his eyes off her. One moment he wanted to shake her; the next, he wanted to crush her against him and kiss her until she stopped fighting him so ferociously and turned that energy into response... as she had done once before.

He wondered if they'd heard about the disappearances of the other prospectors. If they had, would she be so adamant about not leaving? There were so many things about Amador Springs that were wrong. He didn't want either her or her sister to get involved with them. They were so vulnerable so far out of town. When he started to speak, she cut him off.

"I don't expect you to understand. I don't expect anyone to. But Melanie and I are staying here—on our claim—no matter what happens. We have to. And... and when whoever it is sees that we're not going to be driven away, they'll quit harassing us."

He was quick on the uptake. "Something else has happened?"

Linda wanted to bite her tongue. He'd had no idea until she'd given it away. "A few things have gone missing," she said dismissively. "That's all."

"Seems like it's escalating."

Linda shivered. The warning reaction to danger was unseen, but it was definitely felt. Still, she held her ground. "We'll survive," she assured Tate.

"I hope so," was all he said. Yet the simple words stayed with her as he held her gaze for a long moment, before moving away to the upper clearing to answer the call of the Jeep's two-way radio, which had crackled into life and called his name.

I hope so, he'd said. She hoped so, too. Was she doing the right thing? For herself, yes. But for Melanie?

She started to call after him, to stop him before he disappeared from view. His tall form was fast moving away from her. He was almost beside the tree. She knew that with one word from her he would turn and...

The word never came. She couldn't utter it. It caught in her throat and wouldn't be said, because suddenly she was hit with the realization that it was she who wanted to be taken care of, to be protected. And it was Tate she wanted to cling to.

The moment didn't last long. At least, she didn't let it last long. Within the space of two breaths she had herself back under control. And if by chance he *had* turned to look back at her after stepping under the spread of the gnarled old oak's heavy limbs, he wouldn't have seen any trace of vulnerability left in her expression.

Linda didn't wait to suffer another onslaught of emotion. She needed to keep to a steady course. She couldn't let herself become sidetracked, either by fear or by attraction to a man.

Chapter Nine

Tate's jaw was set as he nodded to Patrick and took a seat at the empty desk across from him. Things were certainly beginning to add up. To what, he wasn't sure. There seemed to be more confusion than clarity. But somehow there was a connection.

Were the people responsible for trying to drive Linda and Melanie away from their claim involved at all with the disappearances? Had they mounted just such a campaign against the others? But if that was so, why had no one made a complaint? Then he thought of Linda. If he hadn't come upon the fresh evidence at the scene, she would have kept the information to herself in the hope that whoever was responsible would stop. But would they stop? Or would they rely upon each prospector's natural reticence? Was that their ploy? Escalate the harassment to the stage where people became afraid for their lives, and the claim would be theirs? Then all they had to do was fade into the surroundings anytime anyone came near?

Patrick cleared his throat, drawing Tate's attention. "Something up?" he asked.

Tate pushed himself to his feet, unable to remain still. He walked to the window to look out on a scene that was deceptively sleepy. No one seemed to be moving in the old town. Not a person, not a dog. "I stopped by the Conway claim this morning. Someone had slashed the tubes on their dredge."

Patrick sat forward. "Slashed, you say?"

Tate nodded, looking from the street to his old friend. Patrick was frowning, his face drawn in dark consideration. Tate met the suddenly perceptive gray eyes. "Did a good job on them, too. No way to think it might have been an accident."

"Did either of the girls see who did it?"

Tate didn't think Linda Conway would appreciate being referred to as a "girl," but Patrick was of another generation, and this was no time to be considering the possibility of aggrieved sensibilities. "I talked with Linda," he answered. "She heard something in the night but didn't see anyone."

Patrick didn't say anything. Instead, he reached for the gun and holster that he usually left hanging on one finger of an old hat rack. As he started to strap on the holster, he said, "Guess maybe we'd better get out there and check things out."

Tate stopped him. "I don't think that would do any good right now."

"Why not?"

"Because I doubt that we'll find anything. Whoever's doing this is obviously very careful."

Patrick's eyes narrowed. "You think it might have something to do with the disappearances?"

"Don't you?"

"We don't have anything else to go on. With the others, it's as if the earth opened up, took a swallow and didn't leave a clue. If there *is* a connection, this might be our first break."

Tate's lips thinned. As he turned back to the window, he saw Roland Barns making his way across the street to the office. The man swaggered as he walked...and he always wore his gun slung low on his hip like a Hollywood gunfighter. He might be laughable if he weren't an unknown quantity.

Tate spoke quickly to his friend. "Don't say anything about this to Roland." He didn't know why he had that intuition, but he felt it strongly enough to act upon it. "I'm going to camp out close to the Conway place for a few nights—see what I can see. And the fewer people who know about it, the better I'll like it."

Patrick's frown was quick and the look he gave Tate even sharper than any he had given him before. But there wasn't time for discussion. Roland was already at the door, and all Patrick could do was give a quick assenting nod.

LINDA AND MELANIE returned to the same service station that they had visited their first day in Amador Springs to inflate the replacement tubes they had found in their uncle's collection of spare parts.

The same wiry little old man came out to assist them, his sharp blue eyes running over their faces as he came up to the car. "You two are Roger Conway's nieces, aren't you? I never forget a face. I've been workin' at this station for twenty-five years and I bet I'd recognize everyone who ever came in here. Never forget a face. Never."

Linda stepped from the car and walked to the back to the trunk.

"Fill 'er up, miss?" the man asked, following closely behind.

Linda withdrew the tubes. "With air, yes," Linda replied.

The old man accepted the deflated rubber circles. "Sure 'nough. Air's cheap. Won't charge you a penny for it."

Linda smiled as his crinkled blue gaze invited. If all the old man had to do all day was talk to the people who came into his station, some of his days must be pretty lonely. She walked to the pump platform with him and waited as he released the stem cover and attached the air hose to one tube. A hissing noise followed. Soon the tube was plump and round. He repeated the action on the second tube. When he was done, he carried them both back to her car and stowed them in the back seat. They were now too bulky for the trunk.

"How do you two like prospecting?" he asked, including Melanie in his question.

Linda slid back into the driver's seat. "We like it fine," she replied.

"Hard work," he agreed.

"Have you ever looked for gold?" Melanie asked, attempting to be polite.

The old man laughed. "Years ago I did. But I'm too old now. Too old to get discouraged time after time. I'd rather sit right here and fill people's cars up with this liquid gold. Anyway, it's gotten too damn dangerous."

"Dangerous?" Linda repeated.

"Sure! People disappearin' and such. Here one day, gone the next...no one ever hearin' from 'em again." He shook his grizzled head. "Nope, not for me. I like my hide a little too much." Pale eyes fixed on them. "You two run into any more trouble?"

"Trouble?" Linda asked. Her heart began beating faster.

"Like you did that first day...askin' for the sheriff 'n all."

Linda started the car. "No, no trouble," she replied. She put the car into gear.

"Well, if you do, some people say Patrick McHenry won't do you much good. Some say he can't even help himself. Me? I don't know. I think I'll just sit right here and watch."

Linda accelerated the car without making a reply. From the corner of her eye she saw the man wave, but neither she nor Melanie waved in return.

Melanie waited no longer than a few seconds to demand, "Do you know what he was talking about? It sounded like he was saying bad things about Patrick."

"I'd say that's a safe bet."

"But why?" she demanded again.

"Did you hear what he said about the disappearances? Remember when we first came here? He said something then about Uncle Roger's 'accident.'"

Melanie heard the stress on the last word. "You mean...he was trying to tell us it wasn't an accident? What's going on here, Linda? What's happening?"

"I wish I knew," Linda replied, her fingers tightening on the steering wheel. She glanced at her younger sister. "How would you feel about moving into town?"

"Town?"

"Just for a little while. A few days, a week."

"What about you?"

"I'm staying at the claim."

"Then I am, too."

Linda closed her eyes, instinctively keeping the car on course for a few seconds before she opened them again. She had fought against Tate Winslow's similar suggestion earlier that morning. Even then she had wondered if she was doing the proper thing. Now she was even less sure. But one of them had to stay. If they both left, the men would return and Melanie and she might not get their claim back.

"I'm not the one who's been ill," she said at last.

"Am I going to have to pay for that forever?" Melanie's painfully worded question cut deeply into Linda's heart, the anguish behind it giving a ragged edge to the words. They both knew that illness wasn't the cause. Not simple illness. And they both knew that Melanie wasn't only referring to her own physical devastation. Someone else had been involved; someone who had paid with his life.

The tension tightened in Linda's body. Sometimes she felt so ill-equipped to help her sister. After the accident there had been many doctors, but none had been able to mend the fragility of Melanie's spirit. She would have to learn to live with what had happened. As difficult as that was, she would have to find the strength.

Only now she had little strength to draw from...and what strength she found, she borrowed from Linda.

Linda steeled herself to the task, unconsciously giving, unselfishly loving. Whatever the outcome, they would stay together.

"If you don't want to go, you don't have to. Okay?" she promised.

Melanie shivered. Part of her wanted to flee to the relative safety of the town, the other part of her clung to Linda's fortitude. In her she could find herself. Melanie answered softly, "Okay."

The whispered word still held pain. Linda felt it but could do nothing about it. No matter which way she turned, it seemed that she hadn't helped... when all she wanted to do in the world was comfort her sister.

LINDA PERCHED at the edge of the stream, panning the concentrate from the tub. Time after time her actions yielded nothing, and she was beginning to get very discouraged. It had taken most of the morning to get the dredge back into working condition; replacing the slashed tubes had not been as easy a job as she'd thought. *Nothing* about looking for gold seemed to be easy.

She dipped into the tub for another try, settled the pan underwater and began to swirl it. Then she stopped, blinked and slowly straightened.

In her pan was a chunk of material much larger than anything around it. Much larger and much yellower.

Linda blinked again, not believing the evidence of her eyes. She touched it with a disbelieving finger. The nugget was real. Real!

She wanted to scream. She wanted to shout. Her heart started to hammer, her hands began to shake. She lifted the nugget away from the pan, surprised by its weight. As she cradled it in her fingers, it gleamed golden in the sun.

After all the work, after all the uncertainty... the moment had come! There *was* substantial gold on their uncle's claim. And they were finding it!

Linda continued to stare at the nugget. She knew a silly grin was fixed on her face, but for the life of her she couldn't erase it.

Then, her hands still shaking, she carefully wrapped the piece of gold in a handkerchief and stuffed it into her pocket. When Melanie awakened from her nap, she would show it to her. Then they could both share in the thrill of discovery. They could both be excited and happy and maybe even go into town to celebrate.

However, when Melanie joined her outside, Linda's excitement was dulled by the flush on her sister's pale cheeks and the listless attitude that usually forewarned another bout with illness. For the moment she kept the discovery to herself.

Yet when she went to bed that night, after having made sure that her sister was tucked in tightly, she reached for the evidence of golden promise and held it tightly to her heart. With this and with many more like it, their objective was coming closer to realization. They could keep the ranch... and what was just as important, each of them could slip from beneath the cloak of guilt that weighed so heavily upon their souls. Because if she'd found one nugget, there had to be another... and another... and another....

TATE WRAPPED the old woolen blanket around his long body, just as he had for the past two nights. From the vantage point of the rim of the embankment, he had observed the Conway campsite, keenly aware of any sound or movement. And during that time nothing unusual had occurred. It was enough to make even him question the accuracy of his suspicions.

Tate settled his head against his crooked arm. Tomorrow night he doubted he would be able to come. Patrick was fast succumbing to a bad cold and was only hanging on by will alone, and Roland had sent word that afternoon that he was ill, as well, which would leave only himself to act as sentinel for the town. He couldn't spend his nights at a claim, especially one where nothing was happening. He only hoped the situation would not change.

LINDA COCKED HER HEAD, straining to hear. She had been awakened by something walking next to the lean-to's wall.

For the past three days and nights they had enjoyed a wonderful measure of calm. Did this mean that their time of peace was over?

She heard the sound again. It was close. She could hear whatever it was breathing. Then an unearthly cry caused icy chills to run up and down her spine. The cry came again, vividly lethal on the other side of the flimsy structure.

Linda reached for the stout piece of pipe she had brought inside. Her fingers wrapped around it like a caring friend.

She glanced at Melanie, who was stirring restlessly in her sleep.

Linda waited. Nothing. She waited longer. Still nothing. She might never have been disturbed from her sleep, so deep was the ensuing silence.

Slowly she lowered herself back into her sleeping bag and pulled the cover to her chin.

Whatever it was might have gone...but just in case, she kept the pipe clutched tightly in her hand.

DEEP COUGHS racked Melanie's frail body the next morning, coughs that failed to completely clear her lungs.

Linda shrugged away the repeated apologies. She was worried about her sister. Her condition seemed to be worsening.

Finally she announced, "We're going into town."

"Why?" Melanie asked.

"Because we just are."

Not giving her sister time to form a protest, she bundled her up against the cool of morning and drove them into town to the general store, where, if they couldn't locate a doctor, they could at least find something that might help.

This time Melanie came into the store with her, insisting that she not be any more of a burden than she already was. Because she looked to be on the verge of tears, Linda agreed.

The woman who ran the store gave Melanie an all-encompassing glance when she coughed. "I have just what you need right here," she said, leading the way to a counter where a number of small bottles were standing. "This works miracles."

Linda looked from the bottles to the woman's kindly face. "I was really wondering about a doctor—"

Melanie grasped her arm. "Not a doctor, Linda. Not again. Please!"

The woman regretfully shook her head. "Doc Peters is the closest, and he's gone to some kind of convention. He told all of us to go to a doctor friend of his in Sacramento, if we needed him."

Melanie's hand tightened on Linda's arm. She looked pleadingly into her sister's eyes.

Against her better judgment, Linda gave in and bought a bottle of the "miracle" medicine.

To her surprise and relief, by the next afternoon Melanie was better. And when the bottle was empty, she felt almost well. At Melanie's suggestion, they went back into town for a refill.

WHEN THE SISTERS ARRIVED, Roland Barns was in the store, leaning against the counter.

The storekeeper smiled upon hearing of Melanie's progress and went with her to the counter where the curative was kept.

Roland, taking advantage of the moment, sidled up to Linda, a smile lurking beneath his mustache. "Dona can fix your sister up good. She did me. I've been sick, too, but a few shots of Dona's specialty had me right back on my feet. 'Course I'm not back at work yet. Thought I'd take a few more days off. Tate seems able to handle things." He laughed, as if at a none too friendly thought. "Patrick's been under the weather, too. Bad cold going around."

Melanie came into hearing range. "Patrick's sick?" she asked, frowning.

Roland nodded.

Melanie immediately turned pleading eyes on Linda. "We have to go see him, Linda."

Roland laughed again. "Oh, he's all right. Tate's been looking after him. If you ask me, he likes to look after him... maybe a little too much."

Linda caught the smoky drift of Roland's words and she didn't like the direction they were taking. "What are you trying to say, Mr. Barns?"

"Roland," he corrected and grinned. "And I'm not saying anything."

"It sounds to me as if you are," Linda answered stiffly.

Melanie looked at them in confusion.

Roland glanced at her sister and then back at Linda. "Not me. I leave other people to live their lives exactly as they want."

"Whose lives? I don't understand," Melanie complained.

The woman who owned the store came back from bagging the squat bottle. "That'll be $3.95."

Linda dug the money from her pocket and placed it on the counter. She shot a glance of dislike toward Roland and turned to leave the room. She felt Melanie look from him to her and then follow her.

Roland's voice was smooth as he called, "Don't say I didn't try to warn you."

"Warn you about what?" Melanie asked as they crossed the sidewalk toward the car.

Linda's back was so straight a ramrod could have been welded to her spine. Her face was rigid, too, as she turned to her sister after they both had settled in the car. "The deputy was trying to intimate that Tate and Patrick are a couple. Understand?"

Melanie blinked. "No! That's not true. Why would he say something like that?"

"I think he's jealous."

"Because of you?"

Linda frowned and ran a hand through her hair. "No, not because of me. I don't enter into it. Neither do you. I think he's jealous of something else."

"Like what?"

"I don't have any idea."

"Should we tell Tate?"

"Maybe this is the first time Roland's said anything like that to anyone. He was careful that only we heard him."

"I think he's an awful man."

"I do, too."

Melanie was silent as Linda started the car. Then she asked softly, "Can we still drop by to see Patrick?"

Linda arched an eyebrow. "Do you feel well enough?"

"Yes."

"Then let's stop by, but only for a few minutes. We'll see if there's anything we can do to help him."

Melanie smiled happily, already putting from her mind the sly intimation she had heard only a moment before.

PATRICK WAS EMBARRASSED by his weakened state when he discovered that he had visitors.

"I'm not usually such a weak Nelly," he said, trying to clear the clutter from the living room. "Or such a bad housekeeper."

"We didn't come to see your house," Melanie said softly.

"Still—" He only succeeded in straightening the newspapers strewn around his chair before being overcome by a series of coughs that caused him to sink back onto the cushion. When he could speak again, he said, "Tate should be bringing my lunch in a few minutes. I'll ask him to get you something to drink. I have instructions not to try to fix anything myself. Can't think why. I've been doing it all my life."

"Maybe Tate wants you to rest...to help you get well," Linda suggested.

Melanie, sitting across from him, asked, "Have you tried the medicine the lady at the general store recommends? I've been sick, too, and it really helped."

"Stuff knocks me out colder than a mackerel. I'd rather be sick than comatose. I think it's got some kind of added kick...like eighty proof alcohol! Every time I get a sniffle, Dona always tries to pawn her brew off on me. I think I've finally got her convinced that it's a losing battle. Probably should arrest her for selling medicine without a license, but she gets around it by saying it's herbal. And half the area would revolt if I did—seems to help a lot of people."

Melanie pushed the bagged bottle deeper into the side pocket of her purse. "It really did make me feel better," she said quietly.

Patrick smiled. "Then that's another reason not to arrest her. If she can make you feel good, I'd say she's doing quite a service."

Melanie flushed slightly but was happy with his words. She smiled into his eyes, feeling the kindness of the man.

The front door opened and closed and Tate came into the room carrying a covered tray. He was surprised that Patrick wasn't alone. He was particularly surprised by the identity of his guests.

Linda immediately stood up. "We'd better go," she said to Melanie.

"No...no, stay," Patrick urged. "I'm not really very hungry."

Melanie agreed with her sister. "No, we only came to see how you were. And to—" She crossed the short space between herself and the older man and leaned down to give him a quick hug.

Was she missing their father, too? Linda wondered. She had to be. They both did.

When Melanie straightened, a haze of tears was in her eyes. "You just take care of yourself. And do what Tate says. I know we haven't known each other long, but I like you. And—"

Linda helped her sister when she seemed at a loss for words. "And Melanie has to rest, too. We just came into the town for more medicine." She glanced at Tate. "She's been ill with this cold, too."

Tate tried to read the expression in her eyes. He knew there was a message deep within them, but he was momentarily at a loss to know what it was.

He saw them to the door after having put the tray on a table beside Patrick. The two women called their goodbyes and stepped onto the porch. Tate followed.

"You haven't had any more trouble, have you?" he asked.

Linda thought of the animal's visit. Now that time had passed, she was slightly ashamed of her cowardly behavior. The animal probably had wandered into their camp by pure coincidence, looking for food or something. A free handout. She shook her head. "No, not a bit."

Her delay in answering stirred Tate's suspicions. He wouldn't try to get the truth from her now. Not here. Not with Melanie having to reach out to the porch rail for support. But he would ask her soon. And he hoped to make her see that telling the truth could be one of the more important actions of her life.

He assisted Melanie to the car, and she bestowed such a warm smile on him that Linda's withdrawal was obvious by comparison.

LINDA WORKED the stream with renewed vigor the next day and was rewarded with a nugget almost the same size as the first. This time she showed both to Melanie.

Melanie's eyes grew large at sight of the gold. "It's happening, isn't it?" she whispered, lifting her eyes in awe.

Linda grinned. "I think it is. Of course, we have to find a lot more."

Melanie moved the gold pieces around in her palm. "I was afraid—"

"So was I," Linda admitted. "I still am sometimes. This seems so much like a dream. But it's not a dream. That gold is real. And it's going to give us everything that we want!"

Melanie stared at the gold. What she wanted, gold couldn't give: it couldn't bring back a life. But she kept the thought to herself. Linda had worked so hard. She wouldn't take away her joy with a thoughtless word. She started to hand back the nuggets.

Linda shook her head. "No—you keep them. I might drop them in the stream or something."

Melanie carefully wrapped the nuggets in the handkerchief. "I won't lose them, I promise."

"I know you won't," Linda agreed, then smiled at her sister before going back to work.

TATE WAS TORN between his call to duty and his desire to confront Linda Conway. To Patrick he confided nothing, because if he did, the older man would hurry his recuperation and try to return to his job too soon. And at Patrick's age that wasn't a good idea.

Of Roland Barns he saw nothing until late the next afternoon, when by chance he ran into the man talking with a small group of men who had come in from their claims and were standing outside the general store.

When Roland saw him, he didn't pretend to be ill any longer. He broke away from the group and swaggered over to Tate. "I was just on my way to see you."

Tate didn't return the deputy's wry grin. "I thought you were too sick to get out of bed."

"I'm better, as you can see. I was coming to tell you that if you need me to take my shift, I can."

"Were you now." Tate had seen too many students tell the same sort of lie not to know when an attempt was being made to deceive him. If he hadn't seen Roland, the deputy wouldn't have come in for as long as he thought he could get away with it. Tate wondered if the man had been ill at all. Or had he just taken a short vacation at Tate's expense? His tone was dry as he replied, "Yeah, I could use a little help."

"Patrick still sick?" Roland asked, raising his voice ever so slightly so that the men nearby could hear.

Tate's lips tightened. He didn't know the game Roland was up to, but his first instinct that the man was no friend of Patrick's had intensified. "He's getting better."

"Seems to be hanging on a long time. That's too bad."

Tate silently ground his teeth. *Make Patrick look physically incapable of doing his job as well as inept.* That was just what Patrick needed. The small group of men murmured softly among themselves. "He's a tough man. He'll be back in top form soon."

At that moment Mrs. Armbruster came out of the store and her eyes swept over the deputies. She marched directly to Roland and said, "I'd like to have a word with you. Whenever you're free." She dismissed Tate by not acknowledging him.

Roland smiled silkily. "Why, of course. I'm free now, I believe. Tate, you don't mind if I'm a few minutes late getting to the office, do you?"

Tate's answer was strained. "Take whatever time you need. But be there by five."

Roland checked his watch. "Sure... no problem." He shepherded the woman toward the café, and as they moved across the street was heard to say, "Now what can I do for you this nice day, Bertha?"

Tate focused his attention on the group of men standing a short distance away from him. Some of them he remembered from childhood. They had been living in the vicinity of Amador Springs that long. A few had come later. But, like Mrs. Armbruster, he knew the newcomers had quickly been informed of his past. And the knowledge stung. He was sure the stories had grown over the years. Even if they hadn't, they had been bad enough as they were to make good fodder. The passage of time would not dim them.

Once, Tate might have looked quickly away—the sins of the father visited upon the son. But the past was the past and one day had to be buried. He kept his eyes steadily on the men, refusing to be intimidated. This time it was the others who looked away first. The little group broke up slowly, each man going a different way, some pushing past him without a word, others looking at him as if they wanted to say something but deciding in the end not to do so.

Alone in the street, Tate took a deep breath. Somehow he felt as if he had survived a test.

Years had slipped away. Time had curled in on itself and he might have been the skinny young boy angrily fighting against the town as well as his father—and getting slapped down in the process by both. The child who wanted so desperately to be proud of his only parent, yet was achingly locked in defeat.

Tate slowly relaxed the fists he had unconsciously made. This time he had won. The battle might seemingly have involved the others, but he knew that it had been fought mainly within himself. And it was within himself that he now felt a measure of peace begin to dawn, for the first time in all his adult life.

Chapter Ten

Linda picked up a small stone and morosely tossed it into the stream. She didn't understand why she was having to force herself to be happy. She should still be excited, pleased, exuberant, shouldn't she? They were starting to find the gold they had hoped for...the gold that was going to solve all their problems. At least she had thought it was going to solve their problems. Now she wasn't so sure.

She reached for another stone and tossed it into the water, as well. She wished Melanie hadn't gone to sleep so early this evening. With her she could pretend to a measure of surety. On her own, she was falling prey to emotions that suddenly seemed to overpower her. Just who did she think she was to take this burden on herself? To take two lives and wrest reparation from the earth. To try to save a ranch that she sometimes secretly wondered if either of them would be able to keep as the years went by. A land they both loved, yet was it an albatross around their necks, demanding everything and giving little? *No.* She shook her head. The ranch gave to them. It had given to them all their lives. It helped them to have a sense of time and place, because in its soil were the blood and sweat of generations of Conways. It gave them identity. Now it also gave them purpose. They couldn't let it be taken from them, just because one of them was momentarily weak, and the other...

What was she? Strong? Weak? Able? Unable? Sometimes she felt herself to be all of those things. She could act with assurance, talk with assurance, but the basis was terribly hollow. Her life, her responses, counted for little more than a sham, and purely because of times like this. Times when she knew the reality of her own need. When she knew that just because Melanie relied upon her for guidance, it didn't mean that she didn't need guidance herself.

A sound that was halfway between a laugh and a sob was torn from her throat. She should be happy, but she wasn't. And she didn't think that she ever would be again. Not if they found all the gold in the river; not if the ranch was theirs to keep for ever and ever. Not even if Melanie suddenly got well, and the terrible oppression that weighed upon her sister was magically lifted.

Linda drew a shaky breath and dropped her face into her hands. She didn't know what was the matter with her. She felt all jumpy inside, restless. When the silent loneliness of the miniature canyon gave her no answer, no release, warm tears began to fall. She was so tired—of pretending to be strong, of pretending to be the one who had all the answers. Her shoulders began to shake at the depth of her desolation.

The crunch of footsteps on gravel caused Linda's head to snap up. At first all she saw was a tall form moving through the haze that blurred her vision, and reacting instinctively, she jumped to her feet in search of a weapon. If it was one of their assailants, she wanted to be prepared. She rubbed at her eyes, trying to clear them. Slowly the form took on an identity, and a familiar voice spoke her name.

"Linda... don't get so upset. It's only me, I'm not going to hurt you."

Linda's fingers tightened on the large rock she had chosen from among many smaller ones. Then slowly her grasp loosened and the rock dropped back to the ground.

Tate's eyes swept over her, seeing the way she tried unsuccessfully to cover the evidence of her tears. He watched as she brought herself to order, pulling herself back into the persona he was more accustomed to.

The realization that she had been crying hit him hard. He wanted to reach out to her, to bring her into his arms for protection, for caring... because he... Because he *what*? His mind skittered away from the answer, then returned. It was almost too incomprehensible to contemplate. He couldn't love her. He barely knew her.

Linda was uncomfortable with the drawn-out silence between them. If he had to intrude upon her private moment, why couldn't he say something? She was determined not to pay any attention to the skip her heart gave upon recognizing him, or the way her breath lightened when he said her name. She was also determined not to remember the last time they had been alone together here at night. But trying not to think about it raised the subject even higher in her consciousness.

"Do you specialize in sneaking up on people?" she demanded, covering for her weakness with an attack.

"I'd hardly call it sneaking," he defended himself.

Linda shot a glance at him through the fading light, then quickly looked away. For want of something to do, she stuffed her hands into her pockets and grumbled, "I would."

Tate relaxed a degree. He didn't believe the realization he had just come to. And yet, when he looked down into that determined little face, saw the fire of challenge in her eyes, let his eyes be drawn to the softness of her mouth... He shook off that line of thought. "Next time I'll bring a bullhorn."

"Is there something you want?"

Tate held back the words that sprang to mind. They were too trite, too banal. Anyway, she'd never receive them in the lighthearted manner in which he'd try to deliver them, because they probably wouldn't come out carefree. He might mean them.

"I just came to see how things are with you," he said instead.

Linda motioned to the darkness fast surrounding them. "Isn't it a little late for that?"

"This is the first chance I've had. Where's Melanie?"

"Asleep."

"It's early."

"She sleeps when she feels like it. She's still not completely over her cold."

"Like Patrick. But he's doing much better now."

"Good."

Another silence fell between them. Linda moved uncomfortably.

Tate's gaze moved to the stream that was busily gurgling past, unconcerned with human sensibilities. If people wanted to enjoy it for its beauty, the stream didn't care. If people cursed its coldness and its occasional winter flood, the stream still didn't care. And if two people were standing at its side, unsure of each other, unsure of themselves, it continued to go about its task on earth, giving no notice. For hundreds of years it had kept its course, forming the narrow little canyon, and it would probably continue to do so for more hundreds of years to come. That knowledge, that blending of past with present and future gave Tate the courage to ask softly, "Why were you crying just now?"

The question riveted Linda to the spot. She hadn't thought he'd noticed. The light had been murky when he arrived. "Crying?" she repeated, trying to gain time to form an answer. She couldn't tell him the real reason. She didn't understand it herself.

Tate nodded.

She took a deep breath. "I didn't know crying was against the law."

"It's not."

"So then?"

He took a step closer. "Linda..."

Linda backed away. "Don't call me that."

"It's your name, isn't it?"

Distracted, she ran a hand through her hair. This was getting worse instead of better. Why couldn't the man mind his own business? Hadn't she asked that before? But he kept pushing and pushing.... "I don't see why you're so determined to do this."

"Do what?"

She made a frustrated movement. "This! You just won't leave it alone, will you? You won't leave *me* alone."

"Has something else happened? Is that why you were crying?"

"No! There was an animal...just an animal. That's all. It had nothing to do with—"

Tate caught her arm. He held it firmly yet gently.

Linda tried to pull away from him but found that she couldn't do it. Or maybe it was that she didn't want to escape all that much. "It doesn't concern..."

"Me. I know. But it does."

"Why?" she demanded, tears coming back into her eyes.

The cry echoed in the quiet night. Tate was just as confused as she was. He didn't understand what was happening, or why it was happening. He didn't understand what was passing between them, but knew that something was.

His fingers unconsciously tightened on her arm. When her expression became pained, he immediately released her. He turned back to look at the stream, which was now being lighted by a rising moon. "Maybe I need to tell you a little more about all of this," he said as he kept his face turned away. "I started to tell you the other day, but we got sidetracked." He paused, then began again. "Normally I'm not a deputy. I got involved in this, because Patrick is a friend of mine and he asked me to help. At least, I knew he needed my help. So I came.

"People have been disappearing from here. At least three prospectors so far. Usually no one would think a thing of it. Prospectors come and go. But this time, something seems more than a little funny."

"I've heard about the disappearances," Linda said.

Tate glanced at her. "I wondered if you had. It was only a matter of time. The disappearances seem to be the main topic of conversation around Amador Springs...that and Patrick's incompetence."

"He's not incompetent."

"He hasn't discovered what happened to the prospectors yet. And it's been several months since the first one disappeared."

"But—"

"Which brings us back to you, and to Melanie."

"Do you think the men who were here that first morning might be involved in the disappearances?"

Tate shrugged. "I've no idea. They might just have been passing through. We have no way of knowing anything."

"Then why are you so interested in us?"

"We don't want you to disappear next."

Linda absorbed the information. She had been afraid his answer might be something like that; it was similar to her own fear. "You said people are blaming Patrick," she said quietly. "Is there a reason to? I mean..." She paused, then hurried on, feeling ashamed for even putting the doubt into words. "Do you think he's able to do his job?"

Tate's lips thinned as he looked down at her. "I've known Patrick for most of my life. The man practically raised me. It was due to him that I haven't grown up to be a criminal. Yes, I think he's still capable of doing his job. He's older, but that doesn't mean he's any less of a man."

Linda looked away. "I'm sorry. I—"

Tate sighed. "It's okay. It's only natural, I suppose."

Linda stared into the night, thinking over all that had been said. "I asked you something once about our uncle. Do you think he might have been . . . killed? He can't be one of the missing, because he was found."

Tate smiled slightly at her confused but accurate deduction. "I don't know what to think."

"Does Patrick?"

"Patrick has enough on his shoulders without asking for more."

Linda was silent a moment. "He's very special to you, isn't he?"

"He's like a father to me."

She thought of Roland Barns's vicious insinuation and suddenly burned with resentment against the man. How could he have said such a thing? She hadn't believed it. But what if she had? He certainly seemed an odd sort of person to be a deputy. She wondered if she should tell Tate what he'd said, but decided against it. Tate must have grown up in this town, and Patrick had been here for years. Surely Roland wouldn't have the nerve to repeat his lie to people who were not strangers?

"So maybe now you can see why I've been so nosy," Tate was saying, drawing her away from her thoughts. Not for anything was he going to admit to more.

Linda accepted his words at face value. She had the feeling that there was more to it than that, but shied away from further speculation. They seemed to have worked out a peaceful understanding between them.

She wasn't prepared to sabotage it the moment it was born.

"Yes."

Tate looked at her. "Does that make you more afraid than you were?"

Linda shook her head. "Not exactly afraid."

"Do you understand why I think it would be better for you two to be in town?"

"Are you back to that?" she demanded, now seeing what he had been leading up to. "No. We're staying right here."

"Even after everything I've told you?"

"You haven't told me anything I didn't already know. And there's something else— Wait here." She crossed to the lean-to, went inside, then came out again a moment later. She was carrying a cardboard box. She came to a halt in front of him before opening it. "See?" she invited him. Inside were two small vials containing grains of gold. Nestled next to them on a bed of cotton were the two nuggets that she'd found. "What do you think?"

Tate reached for one of the nuggets, examined it, then exchanged it for the other. After placing it back beside its companion, he said softly, "Looks as if you've hit pay dirt."

Linda smiled brightly. For the moment her problems, her feeling of insecurity were firmly in the past. "Yes, we thought so, too." Then she sobered. "I can't help but wonder if those two men found—"

She needed to say no more. Tate immediately picked up on her worry. He frowned. "Would you like me to camp out here tonight? Outside the lean-to? Roland's been sick, too, but he's back on duty. If anyone has any trouble, they can go to him."

Linda was shaking her head before he finished. "No. No, thank you. We haven't had any trouble in a long time. Just that animal, like I said. And it was probably looking for food."

"I'd feel better if you'd let me stay."

"No!" The word was said more emphatically than she'd meant. She didn't want him to stay, but not from any sense of misplaced pride. She didn't want him to stay, because the idea of him sleeping just outside her door was to her a more dangerous thought than dealing with the thieves.

Tate nodded tightly before wordlessly turning away.

Linda watched him leave. She knew that their moment of understanding had been damaged and didn't want it to be that way. She called after him. "Tate!" He stopped, turned. "Thanks," she repeated uncertainly, lifting a hand in an unconscious plea.

Tate remained perfectly still. Then once again he nodded. Only this time when he turned to leave, his back wasn't nearly as inflexible, and she knew that the wall that had suddenly sprung up between them was no longer present.

MELANIE WAS THE FIRST to notice the intruder the next day. She looked up and frowned at the stranger marching toward them. She nudged her sister's arm and slightly motioned with her head.

Linda stood away from the edge of the stream after placing her pan at her feet. She attempted to arrest the woman's progress with a none too inviting, "Yes, can we help you?"

The woman paid no attention to the warning. She gave the impression of an overblown sort of person, both in personality and in stature. She kept coming until she was at the other side of the stream. Only the narrowness of the crossing board gave her pause. She looked from it to the sisters. "You can help me a great deal, actually."

"In what way?" Linda challenged her.

The visitor withdrew a folded sheet of paper from her handbag. "You can add your signature to this." The paper naturally unfurled as she thrust it forward. Of course, she was too far away for either of them to read the wording, but that didn't seem to concern her.

Linda's frown was darkening as her impatience grew. "What is this all about?"

"It's a recall petition. I'm going around to all the claims in the area to ask for help in getting Patrick McHenry turned out of office."

Linda felt Melanie stiffen. "Would you like to tell us why?" she questioned.

The woman didn't hesitate. "Because the man is incapable of doing his job. He's old, he's incompetent, he's—"

"He's our *friend*!" Melanie interrupted, a flush of color on each pale cheek.

The woman wasn't impressed. "That may well be, but it doesn't change any of the facts."

"Who *are* you?" Melanie demanded.

The woman's chin lifted. "*I* am Bertha Armbruster. My father disappeared from Amador Springs six weeks ago. I came here recently to try to get some action taken, and I haven't been able to get anyone to budge!"

"I'm sure that's not true," Linda corrected her.

"It is."

"If it is, then there's probably a reason," Melanie broke in.

"Incompetence, that's the reason. Or possibly worse. I have it from a good source that some odd things have been happening in these parts. Some things that the sheriff seems to be turning a blind eye to. Then he brings in that 'friend' of his. I've heard stories about *that*, too. But I won't repeat them. Let's just say that neither Patrick McHenry nor Tate Winslow have any business representing justice. Why, that Winslow man is little better than an outlaw himself."

Melanie started to protest, but Linda cut her off with a quietly worded, "Why do you say that?" to Mrs. Armbruster at the same time as she gave her sister a warning touch. She was curious how far the woman was going to go in libeling Tate.

"His father was the town drunk, haven't you heard? I know you're new to the area and all, but I'd have thought you'd have heard that. Used to disgrace himself regularly. Face in the gutter... all of it. Disgusting. Then the boy—" She drew a breath, almost as if relishing her story. "The boy was wild. And I mean really wild. Tore things up, stole things. People say he and his father were trash. Then he's supposed to have had this big turnaround...that he's now some kind of professor at a college near Mount Shasta. I say it's all a lie. I think more than likely he's been in jail, and that college story is just pure fabrication."

Linda was vibrating with anger. "Do you have any proof, Mrs. Armbruster?" she asked tightly.

"I don't need proof."

"You might, when we tell Tate what you've been saying about him."

"And Patrick!" Melanie added quickly.

Linda continued before the woman could make a reply. "I think you'd better leave our claim. You're not welcome here."

"So you really are their friends. I'd heard that, but I didn't see how you could be, especially not if what I heard about your uncle is true."

"Our uncle had a fall, Mrs. Armbruster."

"So the sheriff says."

Linda made an aggressive move forward. She was much smaller than the other woman, but something in her expression must have persuaded Bertha Armbruster to yield. "So *I* say," Linda gritted. "Now, get out. Get out before I have to..."

"You'll regret this. I promise you, you'll regret it!" Mrs. Armbruster warned as she struggled hurriedly up the embankment.

Linda called after her. "Maybe you shouldn't listen to so much gossip. That's something that can be regretted, too... especially if it's proved wrong!"

The woman made a reply, but neither Linda nor Melanie understood it.

Once they were alone, Linda ran a hand through her hair, and Melanie searched for a spot to sit down.

"My God," Linda murmured. "Tate said Patrick had his troubles, but I didn't expect it to be *this* bad."

"You knew about this?" Melanie asked.

"A little bit."

"She's a horrible woman."

"Probably getting her information from a 'horrible' man. Did you hear what she said about Tate and Patrick? We know where that came from."

"Roland Barns."

"Exactly."

"We should tell Tate."

"I think maybe we will."

Melanie looked closely at her sister. "You've come around to liking Tate, haven't you?"

Linda turned slightly away. "I don't enjoy hearing anyone defamed."

"But you were really angry. I haven't seen you that angry since... I don't know when."

Linda hadn't told her sister about her vivid exchange with the insurance company representative. That was something better left unsaid. Melanie had been fighting for her life then. "The woman's impossible," she pronounced instead.

Melanie gazed into the distance. "She must really care for her father, though. I can understand that."

"So can I, but that's no excuse for her to act as she is. And she's trying to have Patrick recalled. To put who in his place—Roland?"

Melanie turned to her with large, questioning eyes. "Do you think—?"

"I don't know what to think," Linda responded, her lips drawn into a thin line. "But things definitely are more than a little strange around here."

Melanie looked down at her hands.

Linda sighed and turned her troubled gaze to the stream. It seemed as if nothing was simple anymore.

Chapter Eleven

Tate stepped from the shower and rubbed his skin with a towel until it tingled. Then wrapping the towel around his hips, he walked down the hallway to the bedroom Patrick had provided for him upon his arrival.

For the past two nights he had ignored what Linda had said and again bedded down on the outskirts of the sisters' camp, being very careful to keep his presence hidden from them and from anyone else, and leaving each morning shortly before sunrise. That nothing had happened during his time there didn't surprise him—nothing ever seemed to happen if there was a witness. That he had felt such a strong need to keep watch did.

Long hours into each night he had contemplated his tentative discovery, just as he continued to do now. Did he love her? He wasn't sure. Love had played such a little part in his life. He knew he *didn't* love Miriam. He respected her; he liked her, but he didn't love her. He didn't miss her when they were apart. He would be concerned if she was in danger, but he wouldn't feel this driving need to protect her as he did with Linda Conway.

Miriam he knew almost everything about. About Linda Conway he knew almost nothing. Except that he felt something for her that he had never felt for a woman before. She took his determination to exert iron control over every aspect of his life and turned it upside down.

Tate sank onto the edge of the bed and ran long fingers through his damp hair. It didn't help that he was back in Amador Springs, a place he had once sworn never to visit again, doing a job he had no training for while trying to assist a friend he felt almost powerless to help. But he couldn't deceive himself into believing that anything would have been different if he were back at the university and Linda were a fellow teacher or graduate student. The result would have been the same. Setting didn't make this play; the characters did.

Still, he hadn't expected to fall in love. He wasn't even sure he fully approved. Now the question seemed to be: what was he going to do about it?

MELANIE AWAKENED before Linda the next morning, and as she quietly dressed, she smiled at the unexpected turn of events. Then tiptoeing to the door, she slipped outside.

It wasn't often that she was alone like this; since the accident, never. Linda was always there, just as she always had been. First born, almost a second mother—someone both she and her father had relied upon. Only occasionally did Melanie feel any resentment of that fact. Most of the time she was happy not to have had Linda's responsibilities. At times, though—quiet times like this—she enjoyed being momentarily on her own. She enjoyed not having to answer to anyone, not even to Linda...sometimes especially not to Linda, because then she didn't have to feel so guilty. It was bad enough to have taken one life; it was crushing to realize that by her unthinking action she was destroying her sister's life, as well. Linda was working so hard here. For her...for the ranch.

Melanie walked to the edge of the stream. For something to do, she knelt down and picked up a gold pan. She collected some of the material left in the tub and swirled the pan underwater, proud that she was becoming somewhat adept. Then when she lifted it, ready to start the next phase, all motion stopped. Her gaze was trapped by the sight of something golden partially embedded in a mound of clinging debris.

With trembling fingers she rubbed the material away. Then she sat back on her heels, gulping at what she had exposed. It was another nugget! This one was larger than either of the two Linda had found!

For a moment she thought she was going to faint. Her head started to spin, her vision darkened. When the feeling passed, she struggled to her feet and stumbled drunkenly to the lean-to. Her sister's name was on her lips the second she opened the door.

"Linda! You have to wake up! You *have* to!"

Linda came to groggy awareness.

"*Please!*" Melanie pleaded, shaking her.

Linda pushed to her elbows, startled by the urgency of her sister's expression. "What is it?" she asked quickly, trying to compel her mind and body to readiness.

Melanie thrust out her hand. "Look! Look what I've found!"

Linda stared at the nugget, her eyes widening in surprise. "You found that! When?"

"Just now. I woke up early and went out to the stream. Oh, Linda! I can't believe it!"

Linda started to smile. With one motion she threw the top of the sleeping bag off her legs and stood up. "I can!" she said excitedly. With another short series of motions she was dressed and following her sister outside. "We're going to make it, Melanie. We're really going to make it!"

Melanie flashed a quick smile. Both sisters then fell to work, forgetting anything so mundane as breakfast. Also forgetting their intention to go into town to tell Tate and Patrick what they had learned.

LINDA CONTINUED to work the stream long after the time Melanie retired to the shelter because she was continuing to find gold. Nothing as large as the nugget Melanie had discovered that morning, or even the size of her own nuggets. But the findings were steady. Then, as mysteriously as it had materialized, the gold disappeared. Sweep after sweep yielded nothing. Still, Linda continued to work, until darkness made seeing impossible.

Finally giving up, Linda threw herself onto her bedroll and covered her face with her arm. Melanie was already fast asleep, worn out by her busy day. There was no one to see the silent tears rolling from her eyes. Her emotions had gone up so far and then down so low in such a short period of time. In some ways it would have been better not to have had all the promise, because the resulting frustration was too devastating. But, on the other hand, she knew that without such promise, they would be even more discouraged.

Linda sniffed and wiped her eyes. Things would be different if they were just out here for a lark—if they didn't need the money; if they didn't have a definite place for it or require a definite amount. If they were just prospecting for play, they could count the amount they had taken this day as highly successful. But for herself and Melanie, success wouldn't be attained until they had enough to pay off their debts.

Linda turned on her side and closed her eyes. Another silent tear fell to the bedroll.

SOMETHING was chasing her... ready to tear her to pieces if she stumbled! She *couldn't* stumble. It was right behind her! Right... behind...

Linda thrashed against the cover and sat up, her chest heaving, her heart pounding. Her eyes darted to each corner of the room. Then dropping her forehead against her drawn-up knees, she attempted to regain control. The dream had seemed so real.

A moment later she got to her feet, being careful not to disturb Melanie. She had no idea what time it was. Her watch had stopped working, the battery having given its last. She peered out one of the larger cracks in the wall to check the amount of sun. The light was still weak; the hour must be early.

Linda stretched and slipped on her shoes. A quick trip to the outhouse was in order, then she would do as Melanie had done yesterday: go out to the stream and see if she could be as lucky.

She walked softly to the door, opened it, and was preparing to step outside when all the breath was suddenly cut from her lungs. Harking back to her dream, a scream tried to be born. But the sound was held captive by the horror of what she saw.

Linda didn't think that she could move. She felt cold, frozen. Only her eyes bore witness to the fact that she hadn't suddenly become a statue. They were riveted on the doorstep, blinking, trying to deny what she was seeing, trying to make it *be* a dream. But the animal's partially skinned body did not go away.

Her gaze was dragged across the campsite. It was not something she wanted to do; it was a duty she had to perform. As far as she could see, everything else was perfectly normal.

Her eyes came back to the animal. It was a big cat, or at least it had been. A mountain lion. Possibly the one that had come into their camp some nights before. Now it posed no threat. Not in itself. The question was who had killed it, then left it for them to find.

Linda glanced quickly behind her to check that Melanie remained asleep. From the stillness of her sister's form, she judged that it would be some time before she awakened.

Her stomach turned as she once again faced the mutilated carcass. Melanie could *not* see this. It would be more than she could handle. It was almost more than she herself could handle...not from physical revulsion alone, but from the irrefutable evidence that someone really wanted to drive them away. And that that someone was willing to kill. Even if at this moment the kill was an animal, the message was loud and clear. *If you stay, this could happen to you.*

A quake shuddered through Linda's body, only this time not from shock. This time the cause was fear.

"I THINK you should go into town," Melanie said as they sat side by side panning at the stream. "Patrick has to know what that woman's up to." Now that the elation of the day before had mellowed slightly, she remembered their previous plans.

Linda looked up startled. "What about you?" she asked.

"I think I should stay here. You know, keep up a presence. Just in case anyone should get any ideas."

The pan rested heavily in Linda's hands. "No," she said.

Melanie frowned. "No? I don't understand. That doesn't make any sense."

Linda's jaw was set. She shook her head. "No—I don't want you to stay here alone."

"I'll be all right."

Linda silently continued to shake her head.

"Why not?" Melanie demanded.

"Because... I don't think it's a good idea."

"All right. Then we'll both go."

Again Linda shook her head. She liked Patrick. She truly did. And Tate... Linda didn't know exactly what she felt for Tate. She wished he'd just show up like he had before. Then she would tell him about the cougar... and about how afraid she was, even as she steeled herself not to show it around Melanie. "No. I don't think either of us should leave."

Melanie slowly stood up. Reproach was written on her face. "Linda," she chided. "This isn't like you. This isn't worthy of you."

Neither was dragging the dead animal from the doorstep and digging a hole some distance from the shelter large enough to place the animal inside. Nor was erasing all traces of blood from Melanie's sight.

Linda pretended stubbornness. "I don't want to leave."

Melanie's face reflected her disappointment. "The gold's come to mean too much to you. When you place it above people—"

"I *don't* place it above people!" Linda denied, getting to her feet as well. "It's just... I don't think we can really help Patrick. He's got to know what's going on. How can we add anything more to it?"

"He needs to know we're on his side."

"He already knows that."

Melanie looked across at her sister, her pale eyes searching her face. Linda was careful to keep her expression controlled.

"Well then, what about Tate?" Melanie tried again.

"What about him?"

"We were going to tell him what that woman said... about what Roland Barns said."

"That would just stir up trouble."

"Trouble that's not already stirred?"

"I didn't say that."

"But you still won't go."

"No."

"Then I will."

Linda started. Melanie hadn't driven a car since the accident. On more than one occasion she had tried to persuade her to drive, but she had been turned down each time. Now Melanie was willing to take the plunge, but she couldn't let her go. Not by herself. She thought fast, then came to the obvious conclusion. "You can't. You're not insured."

Linda might have hit her so reflexively did Melanie's fragile body crumple. As soon as the words were out, Linda regretted them. She tried to lessen the blow. "I don't think you'd have another accident...it's not that. It's just—"

Melanie turned away. She started to walk slowly back to the lean-to.

Linda wanted to cry out in frustration. Hadn't it been said that whoever loves a person most almost invariably is the one to hurt them the deepest? She hadn't meant to hurt Melanie. She had been trying to save her pain. She ran after her. "Okay...we'll go. We'll both go. We'll tell Patrick and then we'll find Tate and tell him."

Melanie didn't look at her. Instead, continuing to walk, she said quietly, "I've changed my mind. I don't want to go, either. It doesn't matter. Nothing really matters."

The door closed quietly behind her.

Linda remained where she was, her eyes closed to the beauty of the day, her ears closed to all but vilifying self-reproach.

TATE STALKED BACK to the sheriff's office, his jawline rigid, his expression thunderous. For the first time he had just confronted some of the members of the town about the rumors of Patrick's incompetence, and what he discovered merely underscored what he had suspected all along. It was true that several prospectors had gone missing; it was true that acts of random vandalism had occurred sporadically in the town. And it was equally true that Roland Barns was up to his armpits in taking advantage of the situation!

Whenever anyone talked of Patrick's inability to do his job, Roland Barns's name always seemed to enter the picture. Not in an active way. He had been too smart for that. He just had always been there, throwing in a seemingly innocuous comment or two, leading people exactly where he wanted them to go. And no one remembered him saying anything against Patrick.

The game was perfect. Or at least it had been. It wasn't going to be as easy now as it had been before. Tate couldn't prove anything, not yet. But when he could...

Patrick looked up as he entered the tiny office. He was sitting at his desk, a profusion of papers spread out before him, but with a look of such blank misery on his face that Tate knew he had not been working.

Patrick blinked and tried to look busy, shuffling the papers together. "I was just— Paperwork sure piles up."

Tate walked over to Roland's desk and eased himself back against it. He looked at his old friend, at the grayness that hadn't left him after his illness, at the newly formed lines that added years to his real age. "When I first came here, you told me to wait...to keep my eyes and ears open and see what I discovered. Well, I think I've been here long enough to come to a conclusion. Do you want to hear it?"

Patrick's hands stilled. Slowly he lifted his gaze to Tate's. "I guess that depends upon what you're going to say."

"I think it's something you've already guessed. It concerns Roland."

"Go on."

"I think he's causing a lot of your trouble. I don't have any proof yet; this is purely speculation, but I've been talking to some people, and his name isn't usually far from their lips when they start complaining about you."

Patrick stared at him a long moment before saying quietly, "I was afraid of that."

"Why do you keep him on, Patrick? If you've known..."

Patrick shifted in his chair. "I haven't known anything. I've suspected. That's different."

"Still— Why keep him on?"

"Because I don't have any grounds to let him go. And even if I did..."

Tate waited. When it seemed that Patrick was not going to continue, he said quietly, "You're afraid which of you the town might choose to side with. Is that it?"

Patrick closed his eyes. He didn't answer.

Tate's lips tightened. "Amador Springs doesn't deserve you, Patrick."

"Don't say that!" Patrick admonished, his head snapping up, the light of combat in his eyes. He was like a man scorned, who would hear nothing bad said about the woman who mocked him. "Don't *ever* say that. This is my home, Tate. It's been my home for longer than you've been in this world. I've seen people come and I've seen them go, and I've dealt with my share of trouble. But through it all, Amador Springs—"

He had to know. Tate interrupted, saying, "They've started a recall petition."

Patrick took the news like a blow. The breath hissed from his lungs as he fell back in his chair. He looked in danger of collapse.

Tate stood away from the desk, ready to come to his friend's aid. He shouldn't have just come out with it like that. He should have cushioned it more.

The grayness of Patrick's skin had increased. His breathing was labored. Then he visibly collected himself. "I'll—I'll have to talk with them."

"Do you think that's a good idea?"

"I have to do something!"

"Get rid of Roland. If need be, I can put in for a sabbatical at the college. I can stay here longer... through the fall."

Patrick was shaking his head. "No, I can't do that. Not to you. Not to him."

"Why not?" Tate was quick to challenge.

Patrick lifted his gray eyes. "Because I promised the boy's mother I'd help him."

That did put another complexion on the matter. Patrick was helping someone out again. Only this time the procedure was backfiring. "Loyalty can go only so far," Tate warned.

"But we don't *know* that it's him."

"Does he have any idea that he has this stranglehold on you?"

"No."

"Like hell he doesn't!"

"Tate!"

The subject of their gathering argument strode into the office at that moment. He glanced at the other men, took in their strained attitudes and their sudden silence upon his arrival and said, "Sorry, did I interrupt something?"

His fake innocence grated on Tate. "I don't know. You tell us," he snapped.

Roland smiled. "My, my, we are touchy this morning."

Tate made a sudden move forward, a second before Patrick sprang from his chair to grab his arm. "No, Tate. I won't have fighting in this office!"

Roland smirked, which made Tate want to hit him all the more. But the pressure from Patrick's fingers increased, thrusting him momentarily back into childhood—back to all the other times when Patrick had had to intervene in one of his fights. Gracelessly he backed down. The pressure on his arm slowly decreased until Patrick's hand dropped away.

Patrick cleared his throat. "All right. Now..."

"Should I go away and come back again?" Roland asked.

Patrick turned to the sandy-haired deputy. "Maybe that wouldn't be such a bad idea. Come back in a half hour or so."

Roland nodded, his glance sliding to Tate. In it Tate read mocking laughter. His fists tightened at his side. One day he would have it out with Roland. He hoped the day would be soon.

When the other deputy had left, Patrick came around to the front of his desk and patted Tate gruffly on the back. "Sorry to have to do that, son. But it was necessary. Things are bad enough as they are, without it getting around that my two deputies were fighting... and in my office."

What Patrick said was true. But what he didn't seem to realize was the importance of the warning Tate had tried to give him. Didn't Patrick understand how dangerous Roland was to him? And if he did, how could he stand by and do nothing?

Chapter Twelve

The sisters spent an awkward evening. Very little had been said between them since their earlier contretemps. Linda had tried to apologize, but Melanie had withdrawn so far that reaching her was impossible. She seemed not to care about anything, shrugging each time Linda spoke to her, dismissing any effort Linda made to bring harmony between them.

Finally angry, Linda wrapped herself in her sleeping bag and settled for the night. She didn't care when Melanie came to bed. If she wanted to stay up until the wee hours, she could. If she wanted to tire herself out pouting, she could. If she...

Linda's conscience panged. It hadn't been Melanie who had started the trouble, or finished it. It hadn't been she who had spoken unthinkingly.

She bit her bottom lip. Maybe tomorrow things would be better between them. *Give it a night. Let the hours work their magic.* Right now if she tried to apologize again, Melanie would be just as obstinate.

She snuggled closer into her cover and soon after heard Melanie slip into her sleeping bag. Then the light was turned out and the little room was pitched into uncomfortable darkness.

Melanie coughed lightly, once. After that there was only silence.

A SUDDEN BURST of sound echoed through the lean-to, causing Linda instinctively to jerk upright. Her heart had leaped into her throat and her ears were ringing painfully. At first she understood nothing—neither the ensuing thumps and bumps that rained down against the roof and exterior walls, nor the flicker of light seen through the wall cracks that could only mean flame. Then comprehension dawned and she grabbed for her jeans.

Melanie's reactions were slower. She, too, was sitting up, but she had yet to reason out cause and effect. "What—?" she asked muzzily as Linda stood up.

Linda's mouth was dry. "I'm not sure yet. Stay here."

"But—"

"Stay *here*!" Linda ordered. Shock warred with reality. Had there been an explosion? That was the only thing that could explain what she'd heard...what she saw. She reached the door, unlatched it and stepped outside. Caution urged her to stay close to the rough cedar boards, not to rush into the open. But the need to see what had happened drove her to ignore that advice. She hurried around the side of the shelter, then stopped short.

Where the outhouse had stood, there was now only debris. Bits and pieces of it were scattered everywhere. The acridness of smoke and black powder burned her eyes and caught in her throat, while hundreds of tiny sparks danced hotly in the surrounding dry grasses and tried to ignite the parched wood of the shelter.

"No!" Linda cried. Then she started to work on the points of flame endangering the lean-to. Using the closest thing to hand, she gathered loose dirt from the ground and threw it against the burning splinters.

Soon other hands were helping. Melanie was beside her, as she too began to scoop dirt onto the scattered flames. Linda made no complaint that her sister had disregarded her order to stay inside.

Next they turned their attention to the grasses. If these were consumed, so eventually would be the shelter.

Like avenging angels the sisters moved from one spot to another, sometimes using dirt, sometimes using water from the stream.

Their struggle seemed to last for hours.

TATE HAD AWAKENED moments before the explosion, almost as if subconsciously aware of what was to come. When the muted thump of sound pierced the heavy silence just before dawn, he was on his feet and dressing almost before the sound had dissipated.

He knew the direction the blast had come from. In his heart he prayed that the Conways hadn't been involved, but in his mind he knew that the probability was great.

Without bothering to fully button his shirt, he grabbed the unused gun Patrick had given him upon making him a deputy and hurriedly laced his feet into his hiking shoes.

Patrick was standing in his bedroom door as Tate hurried by. "What's going on?" the sheriff asked sleepily. "Did I hear an explosion or something?"

"I think it was. I'm going to check it out."

"Where did it come from? Any idea?"

"I'm not sure. Somewhere east of town."

Patrick saw the tension on Tate's face. "Sure. You go ahead. I'll be there as soon as I can."

Tate didn't answer in words. He merely hurried down the stairs and out the front door. Before Patrick had time to find his uniform slacks, Tate had started his car and was rapidly pulling away from the house.

Sporadic lights sprang on in town. Other people had heard the blast, as well.

Tate's foot pressed down on the accelerator. If anything had happened to Linda or to Melanie...

TATE ARRIVED seconds before Roland. Neither man referred to what had passed between them the day before. Together they ran to the rim of the embankment. And together they stopped, appalled by the damage they saw.

Tate's quick eyes took in the fact that although the outhouse had been destroyed, the lean-to still stood. Which meant that the sisters were probably safe. Still...

Roland started down the embankment, his feet brushing against tufts of ash, causing it to cloud over his boots. Tate quickly followed.

Linda leaned against the outside wall of the shelter, Melanie at her side. Neither of the sisters had spoken.

They looked up, startled, when Tate and Roland crashed into the campsite.

Tate's gaze flashed over Linda before moving on to Melanie. When he saw that they were both unhurt his body lost some of the added tension that had gripped it since he had confirmed that the explosion had come from the Conway claim.

Roland was the first to speak. "Good glory! Are you two all right?"

Linda nodded. After the fact, she found that she was trembling. When she glanced at her sister, she saw that Melanie was trembling, as well. And Melanie hadn't taken time to dress. Her cotton nightshirt fluttered in the cool breeze. Linda's own cotton gown was of little help against the cold and shock, but at least she had pulled on her jeans.

Tate disappeared around the front of the lean-to and soon came out with a blanket that he spread around each sister's shoulders. Linda tremulously smiled her thanks. Tate's hand lingered a little longer next to Linda's cheek. She felt his warmth and was grateful.

He turned when Roland called. The other deputy had moved nearer the site of the explosion. "Dynamite, I'd say. Probably one stick, maybe two. Enough to get the job done."

Tate's jaw tightened. He turned back to Linda and said quietly, "You can't ignore this. If you do, it will be criminal. You *must* move into town."

Linda dropped her head and nodded. Melanie said nothing.

Passages of Gold 183

All the while the sisters packed the clothing they would take, Melanie still remained silent. Linda tried to get her to talk, but her sister uttered not a word.

Patrick arrived at the scene moments before the group left. He told Roland and Tate that he would see them later, that he wanted to stay and have a long look around. They left him poking about the remains of the outbuilding.

IF THE DYNAMITE had been placed closer to the lean-to, their lives would have been over in a second. Linda couldn't shake the thought.

Tate felt her body quiver as he walked with her into the boardinghouse, his arm placed protectively around her shoulders. When he looked down at her, he again experienced the curious blending of love and rage. Love for her—rage against whoever had put her at such risk.

He turned to Roland, who had accompanied Melanie into the room. "Why don't you get their things out of the car? I'll see about securing the rooms."

Roland narrowed his eyes but did as Tate suggested.

The owner of the boardinghouse hurried down a long flight of stairs that were positioned against one wall. He was busy tying the belt around a flannel robe, and his wife was hard on his heels. "What's happened? Did we hear an explosion earlier?"

Tate nodded tightly. "Happened at the Conway place. Think you could give these two a couple of rooms?"

"Sure. No problem." The man hurried around the check-in desk and pulled down two keys.

His wife stood next to the two sisters and made comforting noises. Melanie started to sway and Tate quickly swept her into his arms. "Which room?" he asked.

"No. 5. The other is No. 4. They connect."

Tate nodded and started up the stairs. Melanie's slight weight was as nothing.

Once inside the room, he laid her on the bed. "It'll be all right, Melanie. We'll find whoever did this."

Her blue eyes were wounded. "Does it really matter?" she whispered.

"Of course it matters. It matters a great deal."

Melanie turned her face away as tears flooded her eyes.

Tate stood beside the bed for a long moment, unsure of what to do. Finally he said, "Linda will be up soon. She'll help you undress...or whatever. Probably the best thing for you is to try to sleep."

When Melanie again said nothing, Tate moved to the door feeling helpless.

Downstairs, Roland had returned to drop the suitcases to the floor. To Linda's consternation, he came directly to her and cupped her chin with one hand. She tried to pull away, but he wouldn't let her.

"Don't worry," he said. "We'll find 'em."

Tate appeared on the stairs. His body froze when he saw them standing close. Then he saw Linda try to pull away, and when Roland didn't take the hint, his control snapped. He rapidly completed his descent of the stairs and jerked the deputy's hand away.

"Don't touch her," he warned angrily. "You take your hands off and don't put them on her again!"

Roland smiled. He twisted his wrist out of Tate's grip. "Don't you think that's for the lady to say?"

"The lady is in shock."

"All the more reason she needs help."

Tate lunged forward, then checked himself. Linda didn't need to witness more violence. She had already seen more than enough.

Roland's smile increased. "See?" he said. Then he reached for Linda's arm. "I'll show you to your room. It can't be too far from mine. This place only has five or six rooms suitable to rent, and they're all on the second floor. Which number is it, Tate?"

Tate's hand tightened on the key. If Roland thought he was going to get it away from him, he had another thought coming. "Since I have the key," he said tightly, "I'll see her upstairs."

"And have all the fun?" Roland hectored him.

Linda pried Roland's fingers from her arm. At the moment she'd had about all that she could take. Standing there, hearing them argue was only making things worse. She couldn't hold back her tears much longer. She needed a release. "I'm fine," she said, attempting to take charge of the situation. "Give me the key, and I'll see myself up. Please," she added to Tate when she felt him ready to protest.

He examined her face, saw the determination behind her exhaustion, and handed her the key. "At least let me bring up your bags."

Linda nodded. Then, surprising herself, she turned to Roland and said, "Thank you, Deputy. I—my sister and I—appreciate your help."

Roland Barns looked taken aback, then he collected himself enough to respond smoothly, "Anytime, Miss Conway. Anytime. And remember... I'm just down the hall."

Tate wanted to throttle him. He didn't like the idea of Roland being so close to either Linda or Melanie. But there was precious little he could do about it. They were safer at the boardinghouse than they were on the claim. He gritted his teeth and said nothing. He knew that Roland was just trying to get to him again.

The three ascended the stairs, Tate leading the way, with Linda and Roland following. Tate stopped at Linda's door. She unlocked it, but waited for Roland to pass before opening it. This time Roland took the hint. He tipped his head to Linda, winked at her, then moved jauntily down the hall to the next door. He grinned at Tate as he opened it and went inside. Only a thin wall would separate him from Linda.

Tate tried to control his surging jealousy, amazed that he was feeling such a depth of emotion.

Linda drew his attention as she stepped into the room. He followed her inside, silently setting the suitcases on the floor. He found that he didn't know what to say.

Linda turned to him.

He remained still. Then, almost without him being aware of her movement, she was in his arms, her body pressed against his, her arms wrapped around his waist, her cheek damp against his bare chest where the shirt had pulled partially away.

They remained that way, holding each other, his head resting against the top of hers until Linda drew away. She sniffed, searching in her pocket for a tissue. Finding none, her gaze searched the room. It was an old room, furnished in the style of the previous century. But on the table beside the bed she spotted a box of Kleenex. She removed several tissues and lightly wiped her eyes and nose.

"Thank you, Tate. I—"

"Are you all right?"

Linda gave a wobbly smile. "I suppose...now. I'm sorry I—" She motioned toward him, as if referring to the moments before.

"I'm not," he said softly.

Linda drew a deep breath, then laughed unsteadily with dry irony. "Well, you did always say we'd be safer here. You've been trying to get us into town since the day we arrived."

"I didn't want you to come like this."

"No—"

"Did you see anyone? Hear anything?"

Linda shook her head, remembering the crash of sound that had shaken the shelter's walls. "No...not until the explosion. We were sleeping."

Tate wanted to coax her back into his arms. He wanted to take her to the large bed that was so near and stroke her hair, her body until she forgot the terrible experience of early morning. But he knew that now wasn't the time. Maybe one day. One day when they had all the puzzle solved.

He shifted position and glanced at the connecting door. "Melanie might need you, I think."

"I'm sure she does."

"Did you put the fires out all by yourself? We saw what had happened."

"No, Melanie helped."

He nodded. He hadn't liked the way Melanie seemed so withdrawn. But then he knew that people reacted differently to shock. And if she had helped Linda, that meant she wasn't totally pulled into herself.

"Do you think she needs a doctor?" he asked.

Linda shook her head, remembering Melanie's reaction to her earlier suggestion. "No. She probably just needs to rest."

"That's what I told her."

He was loath to leave. He felt that as long as he was there nothing would happen to her. But if he left...

It was as if Linda read his mind. "We'll *both* be fine. I can't say we weren't startled, but we survived, even if our outhouse didn't."

Tate picked up her flash of humor. He smiled. "It certainly won't ever be the same again."

"Good. I wasn't particularly fond of it."

Tate's smile increased. He glanced at the door. "I guess I'd better go."

Linda nodded.

Still he didn't leave. Finally, taking a deep breath, he closed the door behind him.

Linda didn't want him to go. She wanted him to stay with her—now, in the future, for all time. Quickly she looked away, confused by her sudden discovery. She had known all along that he disturbed her, but she hadn't suspected that it could be more. She knew so little about him. But she knew enough, it seemed. Love didn't demand a wide array of collateral.

His name came softly to her lips as she looked at the spot where he'd been standing.

LINDA SAT on the edge of the bed, her hands twisted tightly together. Morning had slid into afternoon and

Melanie still hadn't shown any improvement. It was as if she had given up. As if Linda's brash, unthinking excuse had combined with the shock of the explosion to extract the last bit of fight from her sister and left her limp. Melanie needed time, she needed peace. She needed to go back home to the ranch.

Linda continued to stare unseeingly at the opposite wall. There was only one way to make it all work, to make everything right again. They had to continue to work the claim, no matter what the danger.

Or rather, *she* had to work the claim. Melanie would be far better off in town...if she could get her to agree.

"OH, YOU POOR THINGS!" Ethyl Tarrant exclaimed upon seeing them the next morning. "You must still be so afraid." The owner's wife was a fussy woman with a narrow face who reveled in gossip. But she was also a kind woman, and the danger surrounding the sisters' arrival had, for the moment, superceded her otherwise natural inclination to pry. "Let me get you some fresh coffee. I've just dished up scrambled eggs, and the bacon should still be hot. And there's fresh biscuits and gravy. My husband comes from the South and he doesn't think anyone can survive without biscuits and gravy. There's also hot cereal and sweet rolls." She paused. "It's too bad you missed Roland. He wanted to see you, but he had to hurry on."

"Yes," Linda agreed, but she didn't mean it. She had purposely waited until she was sure Roland had left for the morning before waking Melanie.

Ethyl Tarrant continued. "Now, if there's anything else you want that you don't see, just let me know."

Linda smiled her thanks, a bit overwhelmed by the array of choices. At the claim their daily fare had been limited. Just as at the claim, there had been no lashings of hot water or a tub in which to soak. At the boardinghouse there were both. She had spent almost a full hour in the bathroom the night before, just enjoying the luxury.

As soon as they were alone, she turned to Melanie and asked, "Did you understand what I said before?" On the way downstairs she had apprised her sister of her plan, but she wasn't sure how much Melanie had absorbed.

"You said you were going back to the claim," Melanie replied. The voice was level, unemotional. Her eyes were fixed inward rather than on anything without.

Linda's hand tightened into itself on the egde of the table. She would rather have an argument than this.

"I think I should. We've come too far to give up now. Especially not when—" She stopped abruptly when the owner of the boardinghouse entered the room. Where his wife was thin, he was round. And his perpetually smiling face was an apt indicator of his sunny disposition.

"Ah—you're not eating. Come on! Come on! You have to have food in order to live. You can't let what happened yesterday upset you today."

Linda felt she had to say something. "We were told when we first arrived in Amador Springs that your wife was a wonderful cook."

He beamed. "She is! I try my hand at times, but I'm nowhere near as good as she is. She's . . . she's—" He sputtered as he tried to think of the proper descriptive word.

Passages of Gold 191

Linda quickly cut in, before he had a chance to get started again. "Mr. Tarrant, I was wondering—" She paused. "Yesterday our car was left at the camp. I'd like to go back and—"

"Get it," he interrupted her, guessing incorrectly. "Of course. I understand." He frowned. "Ordinarily I'd take you myself, but our car is in for repairs at the station. Old Jason said it would take several days." His frown lightened. "Why don't you ask one of the deputies? I'm sure either of them would be happy to take you."

Exactly what she didn't want. She shook her head. "No. Really. I wouldn't want to bother them."

"I'm sure it's no bother."

Linda sighed. She gave the man a level glance. "What I really want is to go back and work the claim."

His frown deepened again. "That wouldn't be such a good idea, would it? From what Roland told us—"

Linda set her jaw. "It's what I want."

The owner slowly began to smile. "A lady who knows her own mind."

"So you see why I'd rather not involve the deputies."

"Of course." He thought for a moment. "Jason might let us borrow his car. I'd still take you, of course. Then you could come back here in yours."

"Wonderful."

"But—" the owner glanced at Melanie and then back to Linda "—is your sister—?" He didn't complete the thought. If Melanie had heard, she might have objected. However, she was in her own world at that moment, a world that had the power to frighten

Linda more than any number of sticks of dynamite, simply because it was a world she could not enter.

"No. Just myself. Melanie is going to stay here."

The man nodded. Then he said, "If you go, you'll stay for the day, right? Not overnight?" When Linda gave a short nod, he continued. "I want you to take my dog. He's the biggest sweetheart in the world, but he's very protective. If I tell him to take care of you, he will."

Linda had worried about protection. Whoever it was seemed ready to play for keeps now. She flashed a quick smile. "I'd appreciate it."

The man beamed again. "I'll go get him. My wife doesn't allow him in the house. She thinks it would offend our boarders. But since he's going to be of help to you—" He hurried out of the room, the look of a roguish child in his expression.

Melanie took a disinterested bite of cereal. Then, as if she hadn't heard the conversation that had taken place around her, she replaced her spoon on the place mat and said, "I'm tired, Linda. I think I'm going to lie down for a while. Are you coming?"

At least now she was initiating conversation between them. Linda had to be thankful for small miracles. "No. I'm going back to the claim, remember? But I'll be back in time for dinner tonight."

"Okay," Melanie said softly. Her blue eyes were muzzy, as if shock still held her in its grip.

She got up from the table and walked smoothly from the room. Linda stared after her. This couldn't go on much longer. If it did, she would be forced to locate a doctor, whether Melanie liked it or not.

Chapter Thirteen

The dog was a huge retriever who answered to the name of Waldo, and who weighed at least as much as Linda did or more. He took an instant liking to her and reared up to cover her face in wet dog kisses. Standing on his hind legs, he was taller than she was.

Linda laughed as she patted his side and tried to bring him under some sort of control.

"He calms down after the first minute," Bob Tarrant declared. "He loves people." He gave the dog a command and the dog instantly settled on his haunches. He looked first at his owner, then at Linda, sensing that he was going to have an exciting day.

Mr. Tarrant handed Linda the dog's leash after instructing him about his duty. From that moment, the dog stuck to her like glue.

THE CAMPSITE was empty when Linda arrived. Mr. Tarrant came with her to check that all was well. It was more his wish than hers.

"Are you sure you want to do this now?" he asked, hesitating to leave.

"I'm positive. And I have Waldo here." The dog wagged his tail.

Bob Tarrant grinned. "That you do. When he gets his dander up, he can make even the most menacing man back down." He reached into his pocket and withdrew something. "Now, I know this isn't exactly legal...." He extended a gun that fitted neatly into the palm of his hand. "It's little, but it's lethal. Do you know how to use one?"

Linda nodded. "Not that type, but..."

"Works like any other." He grinned. "An unbeatable combination—Waldo, you... and this."

Linda accepted the weapon. She broke it open to check the cylinder before clicking it shut with the hammer on an empty chamber. She looked up. "Thank you," she said.

"Just trying to help. Good luck." He waved and started back up the incline.

Linda sighed when he disappeared from view. She pushed the gun into her jeans pocket. She did feel better having it. Then she glanced at the dog. He was sitting across from her, his intelligent face expectant.

"Well, boy," she said. "Let's hope that this is as exciting as it gets."

The tip of his tail flicked. She smiled and motioned for him to follow her.

LINDA HADN'T been dredging for more than an hour when Tate arrived. He skidded down the embankment at a near run, soot from the scattered brushfires of the day before leaving a cloud of smoke at his heels. He didn't alter his speed when he reached the stream. Uncaring of his clothing, he splashed right in to confront her. With one flick of his finger the engine's noise was abruptly cut off.

"Are you crazy?" he accused. "Coming back here all alone? Do you want to get killed?"

Linda rested a hand on her hip, waiting for him to finish. When he did, she said calmly, "I'm not alone."

"You have the dog. I know. I talked with Bob Tarrant."

"And I have this—" She reached past her waders into the pocket of her jeans and withdrew the tiny gun.

Tate's jaw tightened. "At least that's something. Where'd you get it?"

Linda said nothing.

Tate sighed and rubbed the back of his neck. "I still think you're crazy."

"Maybe. But this is something I have to do."

"Why?" He asked the question he had been wanting to ask for some time.

"Do you really want to know?" she challenged him.

He nodded silently.

She waded to the edge of the stream. "Come on. You've got to be freezing."

Tate followed her without comment.

Linda secured the dredge and sat on the ground nearby. The dog came to rest at her side, his great head heavy on her thigh. She patted him absently as Tate stretched out not far away. She postponed the moment by asking curiously, "Are you really a college professor?"

Tate gave her a hooded look. "Where did you hear that?"

"It doesn't matter."

"Yes," he answered after a pause.

"Where?"

He named a college she'd never heard of. "And is it true that you...that you didn't have an easy time of it growing up here?"

"Someone's been talking. I wonder who?"

The bitterness in his tone surprised Linda. She gazed at him curiously. "If it's true, it doesn't make any difference. We don't pick our parents. And they don't pick us."

"It's true," he confirmed, tight-lipped.

Linda nodded. She took a breath and began, "The accident Melanie was in... We...we weren't insured. It was my fault. I forgot to send in the premium. At least, I guess I forgot. Our father had just died and...and I don't remember ever getting a notice, or a reminder. Now we're going to lose our ranch if we don't come up with a lot of money. A man was killed in the accident and his family sued. Then there's the lawyer's fee—so when we got word that Uncle Roger had left us his gold claim..."

"You thought you'd come and strike it rich quick," he completed for her.

"We didn't expect not to have to work!"

Tate leaned forward. He'd seen the way her hands had twisted together as she spoke. "Don't you have any other relatives? Someone you can go to for help?"

She shook her head. "No one."

Tate was silent.

"This is our only hope," she said simply, with the same deep emotion as she had told him everything else.

Tate continued to be silent, his gaze steadily on her.

She didn't flinch away, didn't try to hide behind hostility any longer. Tate was a friend. More than a friend? *Yes, more than a friend.*

He made a sudden move, standing up. "All right. Let's get to work then."

Linda blinked in surprise. "Work?"

"Two are faster than one." He extended a hand. After only a slight hesitation, as she realized what he was prepared to do, Linda accepted it.

AS THE HOURS wore on and they took turns dredging and panning, Tate became increasingly excited by the amount of gold they were finding.

"You're on to something big here, Linda. Possibly really big. That must be why..." He didn't finish his thought, but Linda found it unnecessary. She knew what he had been going to say: that was probably the reason someone was trying to drive her and Melanie away.

Linda continued to work her gold pan in the water. "How much do you think we've found today?"

Tate wiped his forehead. "I don't know. At least a couple hundred ounces."

Linda's hands stopped their motion. She looked up, shocked. "That much? Why at today's prices, that means..."

Tate grinned. "Some people would consider this a fortune."

Linda's face lighted up. Then just as quickly she sobered. They would need so very much more. "We need two weeks exactly like this."

"Surely one would do."

She shook her head decisively. "Half of this is yours."

Tate looked at her through narrow eyes. "I don't remember striking any bargain."

"It's only right. You're doing half the work."

"I don't want it."

Linda stood up, to be on more equal terms with him. "Oh, come on! Money is money. Don't tell me you wouldn't accept it."

"You need it. I don't."

"You're already wealthy?"

He shook his head. "Not on a professor's salary."

"Then—?"

He shook his head again and was about to say something, when in the distance they heard Waldo begin a series of quick, urgent barks. He sounded startled, almost frightened.

For most of the day the great retriever had either slept or played on the bank, sniffing every bush and marking it as his territory. Neither of them had noticed when he wandered away. After a frozen moment, they both started to run toward the sound.

Waldo's barks did not lessen as they struggled through an outgrowth of trees and rocks. When they came to the other side, Tate thrust himself before Linda, shielding her from the unknown danger. Then, taking in the scene, he stopped short. No one was there except the dog, who was barking at something on the ground near the cliff wall.

Linda peered from around Tate's back, surprised by his quick stop. She saw the dog, saw the way the hackles were riding high on his neck, the way his nose was close to the ground and his teeth were exposed as he jerked his front paws from spot to spot. He looked as if he didn't want to be there, yet couldn't leave. He was afraid. But of what?

Her hand unconsciously crept out to clasp Tate's arm. The solidness of it gave her comfort, because suddenly she was afraid, too.

Tate moved forward and her hand slid away. Linda followed closely behind him.

"It's okay, boy. It's okay," Tate crooned softly to the dog, trying to calm him.

Waldo's eyes rolled from Tate back to the ground. He stopped barking, then started up again, just as frantically.

When Tate grabbed hold of the dog's collar, he felt the quivering mass of muscle beneath his fingers. "Waldo!" he said sharply, trying to gain the dog's full attention.

Linda stepped to one side, her concentration no longer on Tate and the dog. Instead, she stared at the slight depression in the earth where Waldo had been digging.

At first she saw material—something blue. Then she saw the withered hand. Bile rose in her throat as she drew a quick breath; instinctively she put up a hand to cover her mouth. But she couldn't turn away. Her eyes were held by the horrible sight. Half buried, half decayed, there was no doubt what lay beyond the little that was showing.

Waldo's barks had turned into keening whines; his body was trembling and his lips were curled in apprehension. An arm around the dog, Tate turned back to Linda, saw the ghostly whiteness of her face and the hollowness of her eyes as she stared at the ground near his side. His gaze moved as well. Then his blood ran cold.

For a moment his mind scattered. He had never seen a dead person before—not one in so grisly a position. He, too, knew what the earth below would yield. He automatically tightened his arm around the frightened animal. Because of that, he received a grateful lick under the chin.

Linda felt her body sway. All at once she was lightheaded. A hand came out to steady her. She looked at Tate and saw her sick horror reflected in his eyes.

"I think—" he began, but had to swallow. "I think we'd better leave now."

Linda couldn't say a word. She merely nodded.

"We'd better get Patrick," he added.

Her shakily drawn breath served as her answer.

THE RIDE into town was fast and silent. All three of the car's occupants were trembling, if not physically, then definitely emotionally. The bag of gold they had gathered was on the floorboards next to Linda's feet. They had taken only seconds to secure the dredge, gather the gold from the containers they had used, and hurry to the Jeep Tate had arrived in. Linda's car was abandoned again.

Tate didn't use the two-way radio because he didn't want to alert any unwanted listeners. So he was forced to witness Patrick's reaction to the news.

Closing his eyes tightly, his old friend looked as if his worst fears were coming to fruition. Then after making several calls, he stood away from his desk, hitched on his gun belt, settled his hat on his head and directed Roland to accompany them.

"Linda stays here," Tate said as they stepped off the sidewalk next to the two county Jeeps that were parked side by side. "She doesn't need to go back there."

Patrick paused. He hadn't been thinking. "You're right. Miss Conway..."

"I want to go back. It—it happened on my land."

Patrick shook his head. "This won't be a pretty sight. And we don't need you now. I'll drop by later to take your statement."

The dog whined at Linda's side. He was tired, upset. And so was she. She looked at Tate. He was tired, too. He tried to give her a reassuring smile, but the effort didn't fool her. He was dreading what they were about to discover—as any feeling man would. Linda let her glance slide away.

"I'll drop Linda off at the boardinghouse, then come right to the claim."

Patrick nodded, getting into the other Jeep. Roland, who had been surprisingly silent, slid into the seat beside the older man. A dark frown had settled on his brow. He appeared not to relish the thought of what was to come, either.

As Linda settled into her seat again, her foot brushed against the bag containing the gold. In their hurry, they had forgotten to secure either the car or the bag. Anyone could have reached in and picked it up. If anyone had walked by... If anyone... Linda's hands came up to cover her face.

Tate started the engine. "Try not to think about it," he advised.

"It's hard not to," she returned honestly. "When I think... He's been there all along, just on the other side of the clearing!"

"Don't!" Tate directed. "It won't do you any good."

Linda got out of the Jeep when it stopped at the boardinghouse. She stepped back as Waldo jumped to the ground. "Do I—? Should I say anything to the others?"

"Not just yet. Wait until we see who it is. It may not be anyone from around here." Even as he said the words, Tate doubted their veracity.

She drew a harsh breath. Her mind hadn't worked that far yet. "Do you think . . . ?"

"I don't know what to think," Tate returned. He jammed the Jeep into gear again. "I've got to go." He faced forward, then turned back to her. His voice softened. "Try not to think about it too much. Okay?"

Linda gave a doubtful nod. She would think of nothing else. "You'll come by later? After . . . ?" She couldn't finish the sentence.

Tate flexed his jaw. "I'll come by," he promised. Then he drove away.

Linda patted the dog as he stood beside her, leaning against her as if for comfort. She would tell no one. Not even Melanie. Especially not Melanie.

TATE TURNED away from the grisly scene, his stomach heaving, wanting to empty itself. Nothing in his life had ever prepared him for this. He swallowed tightly, once . . . twice. The bile finally receded.

Even from where he stood, the stench was awful. He could only thank God that he wasn't one of the men doing the digging. If he had been, he knew that he would have disgraced himself.

He waited beside Patrick and Roland, who watched silently as the crime lab people did their work, then turned the bodies over to the coroner's unit. Not one, but three had been found.

The coroner himself came to talk to them after a time. He was peeling off a pair of rubber gloves. "We'll know more when we get the bodies back to the morgue."

Patrick nodded.

"Got an idea who they might be?" the coroner asked.

Patrick nodded again.

The man sighed and walked away with a weary, "I'll be in touch."

Patrick turned away from the crew of men. He wasn't needed any longer.

Tate glanced at Roland as the two of them fell into step behind the older man. The deputy looked ill, his eyes reflecting his abhorrence of the evidence of the makeshift graves.

None of them said a word as they climbed the embankment to the clearing. Only at the Jeeps did Patrick pause to say, "I'm going off on my own for a bit." His eyes skimmed over Tate to settle on Roland, where they dwelled for several seconds. Then he got into his Jeep and drove away.

Roland stared after him.

He jumped when Tate said, "I'm taking Linda's car to the boardinghouse. We forgot it earlier."

The deputy nodded, but his gaze was vacant. He looked like a man trapped in a waking dream.

He still hadn't moved when Tate, too, pulled away.

TATE WAS EXHAUSTED as he walked through the night, his mind filled with memories that would haunt him for the rest of his life. Not even the shower he had taken after dropping off Linda's car at the boardinghouse had made him feel better—a shower in which he'd had to soap himself down several times to try to remove the feel of the day. He hadn't seen Linda. He hadn't wanted to. Now, seeing her was what he wanted more than anything.

He shuddered at the finality of what had occurred. He had grown up hating Amador Springs, and had left it as soon as he possibly could. But he didn't wish anything like this on the old town. Especially not on his old friend. When word got out, as it probably was doing at this moment, Patrick's life would become even more difficult. Patrick was a proud man, a man who would not back down from anything—unless his pride was taken completely away from him.

Tate had seen what the lack of pride could do. His father had had none. Possibly at one time he had, but when Tate knew him, it was too late. All vestiges of hope had already left the man.

Tate stuffed his fists into his pockets. Coming back to Amador Springs had made him wonder about his father. About what kind of man he had been when he was young. About what once had been his hopes and dreams. About what had tipped him into the life he'd led. Growing up, Tate had often wondered about his mother, speculating on the circumstances of his birth. He had hated his father and despised him for what he was. A boy couldn't look up to a man like that. Not when everyone he knew looked down on both of them.

Tate thought of his father. Tall, bone lean, yet puffy-faced from the drink. He'd never seemed to *want* to be sober. What had he been running away from?

Then he thought of the three prospectors. He hadn't known any of them; they had come to Amador Springs after he left. But he felt compassion for them. Their lives had been cut unnaturally short by a death in which there was little dignity.

He thought again of his father. In death, if not in life, didn't his father deserve a little dignity? And if he couldn't find it with his son, with whom could he find it?

When he first arrived in town, Patrick had told him where his father was buried in the new cemetery on the outskirts of town. Tomorrow, or sometime soon, he would go to that cemetery. He would look at his father's grave. And he would make peace with his memory.

His father had had reasons for the way he behaved. Most people now believed that alcoholism was an illness. Maybe it was. Who was he to say different?

Tate glanced up at the full moon that was helping to light his way. It had been up there, hanging in the sky, circling the earth for how long? Several billion years? It had witnessed many things involving man—many great follies, many great triumphs. As a teacher of recorded history, he knew of most of them. But what of the small follies, the small triumphs that existed only in the souls of individuals? They left no proof, no letters.

Since coming back to Amador Springs, Tate had experienced a great shift in his life. Leaving, he would not be the same man who had entered.

The moon bathed his face in a soft glowing light, highlighting the high cheekbones, the straight nose, the well-defined mouth. His expression was serious.

He welcomed the change.

As LINDA PREPARED for bed that night, she looked into the mirror, not seeing herself, but Tate as she had last seen him. He had been so tired. Still, she had sensed his need to talk as he told her about the growing horror of their initial discovery.

"Three, Linda. There were three of them. The prospectors who were missing—at least, that's what Patrick says. He knew them. I didn't."

"It must have been terrible—for each of you."

"Hardest on Patrick... and will be tomorrow."

"I can't believe they were there all that time... the bodies. When we... When we—"

"It was better that you didn't know."

"Who do you think—?"

He had shaken his head, his expression darkening. Then, shortly afterward, he had gone.

Linda turned out the light and tried to sleep. But sleep was difficult to find when every time she closed her eyes she saw the lifeless hand.

Chapter Fourteen

Linda put off telling Melanie the news, hoping to protect her for as long as possible. But the story must have spread like wildfire in the tiny town. The next morning, on the way to breakfast, they overheard Bob and Ethyl Tarrant arguing heatedly about that very subject.

"I'm going to do it!" Ethyl said firmly. "I'm going to sign that petition. I held off before, but I'm not going to any longer. I doubt anyone else is, either."

"It's not right!" her husband replied tightly. "That Armbruster woman is a troublemaker. I'm glad she moved out of here."

"Three dead men, Bob! Three. And it's not as if they were strangers, which would be bad enough. We *knew* them!"

"Not all that well," Bob qualified.

"They still prospected here."

Bob had been readying something to say in return when he looked around and saw the sisters stand stock-still in the hallway.

"Someone died?" Melanie asked, her voice wavery.

Freshly angry with her husband, Ethyl Tarrant demanded, "Didn't your sister tell you?" She looked from Melanie to Linda. "You were there when the bodies were found. Why didn't you tell us our Waldo had played a big part?"

The dog lifted his head. He was curled in a far corner of the hall, uncertain at this new turnaround. He didn't know that fame had been the open sesame to the house. He flicked his tail at the nearby people.

"Yes, I was there," Linda admitted softly. "For one of them." She felt Melanie's eyes turn on her. They were big and soft and bruised looking. It had taken another shock to bring her sister out of her insular state. "The missing prospectors," Linda explained. "They're not missing anymore. They were—they were buried on our claim."

Melanie's eyes widened. "On our claim?" she repeated, whispering.

Linda nodded slowly. "On the far side of the site clearing—past the entrance to the mine."

Melanie continued to stare at her for another second, then, as if her knees could no longer support her, she began to sink to the floor.

Linda cried out and reached for her at the same instant as Bob Tarrant stepped quickly forward. Melanie half lay, half leaned against both of them. She wasn't unconscious, merely weak. "I'm sorry," she whispered. "It's just—"

"Carry her back to her room, Bob," the older woman directed. "It was the shock of hearing... and she's not strong. I'll make you some nice sweet tea. Does that sound good?" she asked Melanie, motherly concern now on her face. She apologized to Linda. "I'm sorry. I shouldn't have said what I did."

Linda nodded acceptance.

Melanie made no protest against the suggestions. And when their host secured her in his arms, her head fell against his shoulder.

Linda was torn about what to do: accompany Melanie upstairs, or stay on her own where she could think. After yesterday, she had many things to think about.

She watched as Melanie was carried upstairs. Her sister, who relied upon her. Her sister, who looked to her to be strong.

Holding herself stiffly upright, Linda stepped into the parlor where she could be alone.

THE CHAIR Patrick was sitting in squeaked as he sat forward. He cleared his throat. "There's two things I think we have to do. One, set up a full watch on the Conways. Two, get an artist's composite of the men who threatened them. I'll call Sacramento and get someone sent out. I don't think it's a coincidence that the claims of the three prospectors were immediately downstream from the Conways. And considering what's been happening to them since—" He paused. "Those two men, if they are the murderers, know that the Conways are the only ones left alive to have seen them."

Tate nodded. The same thing had occurred to him last night. In his mind there was little doubt about who the murderers were. He knew the amount of gold that was being found on the Conway claim...and since the claims of the missing prospectors *were* immediately downstream, each had had the potential to yield just as generously.

The moment he had stepped inside Patrick's front door from visiting Linda, he had told his old friend of his concern. At first he had wondered how Patrick would react. The day hadn't been easy on him, either. He wondered if he had at last lost heart. But something had happened to Patrick while he was away. A steely glint had formed in his eyes, and the slouch of defeat had disappeared. Even some of the facial lines had rearranged themselves into rugged determination. It was as if the discovery of the bodies had crystallized Patrick's desire to fight.

"How do you want to work it?" Tate asked. "Two Conways, three of us—"

"Do you think the women can be persuaded to stay in one place?"

Tate shrugged. "We can ask."

Patrick turned to Roland. "You're pretty quiet, Roland. Do you disagree with anything I've said?"

Roland looked pale. The dusting of freckles across his skin stood out starkly, and a frown was heavy on his brow. His ability to concentrate didn't seem the best. Patrick had to repeat his question, before the deputy hastily answered, "No...no. I agree."

Patrick reached for the telephone. "I'll make that call. Tate, you go over and talk to the women. They have to be made to see how serious this is."

Tate remembered Linda's face when she saw the hand jutting from the shallow grave. "I think they'll agree," he said quietly.

Patrick nodded. His call connected and he spoke into the phone.

Tate got up. Roland was off in dreamland again. The deputy was staring at him, but he wasn't seeing him, because when Tate moved, Roland's eyes didn't follow.

TATE TAPPED on the door frame of the parlor, causing Linda to jerk around, startled. He smiled slightly. "I can't seem to get this right."

Linda knew immediately to what he was referring: the earlier times when he had startled her and she had struck out against him. But this time she was glad to see him. She gave a slight smile in return. "Come in. I—I want to talk with you."

Tate stepped into the room. "What about?"

Linda's hands came to hold each other tightly. "It's about Melanie. I want to hire some kind of protection for her."

Tate sank down on the couch across from her. "Oh?" She was as anxious as a cat balanced on a loose string.

"I know you'll think I'm being foolish... but I don't want to leave her alone. And she can't come with me. Not now. Now when—"

"Where are you thinking about going?" He already knew the answer, but asked the question, anyway.

Linda's eyes flashed. "To the claim."

He said nothing.

Linda fidgeted. She knew she was acting very foolishly. Whoever was threatening them had killed—not once, but three times. Possibly four, if their uncle was counted in the total. But she couldn't back down. Not when they were so close. "I have to, Tate. You know that I do."

"Patrick wants to give you *both* protection. We still don't know that it was the two men you met when you first arrived, but we think they're a pretty good place to start. And you're the only ones who've seen them."

Linda looked at him.

Tate continued. "He's going to get an artist out here you can describe them to. He wants a picture to circulate."

Linda drew a quick breath. "But I don't remember enough about them to— They were both big. One had a beard, the other didn't. They both had dark hair. That's all I remember."

"That's something."

"But it's not enough!" Linda returned with agitation. That description could fit any number of people.

"Melanie might remember more."

"Melanie's not—" Linda checked what she was about to say.

"She's taking this latest news hard?"

"What do you think?" Linda asked tartly, then quickly doused the flare of sarcasm. "I'm sorry," she said. "I didn't mean to say it that way. I..."

"Just give it a try. That's all Patrick asks."

Linda started to shake her head in automatic denial, when she remembered the position the sheriff had been thrust into. "Things are bad for him, aren't they?" she asked tightly.

"He's holding up—surprisingly well, actually."

A silent moment passed. Then Linda agreed. "All right. I'll try. When should this person get here?"

"In a couple of hours, possibly three. It all depends. Patrick had to call Sacramento."

Linda looked down at her clasped hands. *Three hours.* In three hours she might have lost her nerve to return to the claim.

"Linda—" Tate said her name softly, drawing her gaze. "Really think about it before you go back out there. If you do, one of us will have to come with you, while one stays here with Melanie. That leaves only one person to handle the investigation."

"But the gold!"

"The gold will be there when we're done with all of this. Surely you got enough yesterday to ease things for you for a while. Talk to your lawyer. See what he thinks. It's not worth trading a life for—either yours or someone else's."

Linda chewed her bottom lip. For so long she had focused on only one goal. Postponement seemed unnatural. Yet other people had become involved now. Other lives. "All right," she agreed quietly. "I won't. Not now."

Tate smiled, and it was enough to cause her to catch her breath. His entire face changed when he smiled. The shadow of pain that Melanie had once described to her, and which she recently had seen for herself, disappeared from his eyes. The brush stroke of melancholy shifted to warmth. He might have been a different man... yet he was very much the same.

She tried to look away, but was unsuccessful.

Tate's gaze was held by hers. He couldn't have looked away if he'd tried. And he didn't try. He hadn't expected such quick capitulation. He had thought he'd be forced to much greater degrees of persuasion. That he hadn't; that she'd seen reason and agreed only increased the feeling he held for her. Was it love? It *was* love.

Suddenly he felt detached from everything in the room with the exception of her. The walls with their antiquated paper, the furnishings that belonged to another age, the heavy curtains, the faded carpets on glossed wooden floors...they might not have existed.

A giddy light-headedness took hold of him as a jolt of pure joy shot through his system. At the moment it didn't matter whether she reciprocated the feeling or not. Just to experience it was a gift. Some people went their entire lives without knowing such exhilaration.

Patrick came into the room at that moment, Ethyl Tarrant close on his heels. He drew to an abrupt halt when he saw them, sensing that he was interrupting something important. If he could have left without them noticing and returned later, he would have. But the woman, who had greeted him at the front desk with complaints and had followed him into the room with more, broke the moment with a sharply worded, "People are frightened, Patrick. You can't just ignore that!"

The spell between Linda and Tate was shattered. Each turned to look at the people in the doorway, their expressions dazed.

Patrick gritted his teeth and growled, "I know they're afraid, Ethyl. I'm not senile yet!"

"Well—*do* something about it!"

"If everyone would leave me alone so that I could, I would! Back off, Ethyl. And tell everyone else to give me some room, as well...*and* some cooperation.

Everyone wants me to solve what's going on around here, but no one wants to talk to me."

Ethyl blinked at Patrick's spunk and determination, clear signs of a return to his older self.

Patrick nodded to Tate and Linda. "Excuse the interruption. I came to tell you that the artist will be here in about a half hour. I was able to pull some strings and get some fast action." He gave all his attention to Linda. "You think you and your sister can help?"

A tinge of color was in each of Linda's cheeks, but by this time she had her brain in working order. "I can't make any promises, Patrick. We'll try, but—"

"That's all I expect."

Ethyl Tarrant hadn't moved. She was staring at Patrick and Tate and Linda as if they were players on a stage and she the sole audience. Tiring of her silent role, her tongue suddenly came back to life. "Your sister's asked for some breakfast, Miss Conway. I thought you might like to know."

Linda nodded her thanks.

Patrick's gaze sharpened. "Where is she?"

"In bed," the landlady was happy to answer. "Frightened half to death."

"No," Linda hastily intervened, trying to reassure Patrick. "It's not that. That's not the reason why she..."

"She fainted when she heard the news," the woman protested.

Patrick put his hands on Ethyl Tarrant's shoulders and turned her toward the door. "You said something about her being hungry. Don't you think you should start getting it?"

"In my own house!" the woman huffed. "I don't know who you think you are, Patrick McHenry."

Patrick smiled. "The same person I've always been, Ethyl. Exactly the same."

LINDA CONCENTRATED on the face that was evolving under the skilled fingers of Patrick's police artist from Sacramento. "No—" she murmured regretfully. The woman adjusted her pencil sketch to make the nose a little longer. Again Linda shook her head.

The artist glanced at Melanie, who leaned closer.

Linda worried her bottom lip. She felt so inept! But her memory was so clouded. In the beginning she had seen no need to mark the men's features clearly in her mind; and after being threatened, she had been too afraid.

Melanie shook her head as well and the artist tried again, continuing to question them while she adjusted the forehead, the eyes....

A half hour later, frustration reigned in the room.

As the artist prepared to leave, Linda apologized. "I'm sorry. I just—" She could neither confirm or deny the validity of the drawings. They seemed somewhat familiar and yet—

Patrick rejected her need to apologize. "You've done the best you can," he said. "That's all anyone can ask of you." He turned to Tate. "What we need to do now is get these likenesses around. They may not be totally accurate—" he had hoped for more "—but things like this often jog people's memories. You want to come with me? Roland will stay with the ladies. I told him to meet us here."

A plan had been forming just under the surface of Linda's consciousness. "I'd like to come," she said. All eyes in the room turned to looked at her. "Really, I would," she continued. "I can be of help." She motioned to the drawings. "I don't remember them well enough to describe perfectly, but I'd certainly know them again if I saw them...if we happened upon them."

Melanie started to walk away. Suddenly Linda felt guilty. She hadn't thought to ask her sister if she needed her. "If you want me to stay, Melanie, I will," she offered.

Melanie shook her head. "No...go. The sooner this gets over with, the sooner we can go home." Without a smile she moved into the hall.

Patrick and Tate exchanged glances.

"Is she not feeling well again?" Patrick asked.

"It's nothing physical," Linda answered tightly. "It's just—she's remembering things she'd be much better off not remembering. Part of it's my fault, part of it's hers...and part of it is what's happening here now. There's nothing anyone can do," she added, cutting off any offer of aid they might make.

Neither man said anything.

A few minutes later Roland arrived at the boardinghouse to stand watch, while Linda, Tate and Patrick began a search of the area like none that had been done before.

Chapter Fifteen

Melanie came to awareness stretched on top of the cotton bed cover, a warm breeze drifting across her body from the partially open window at her side. She had no idea how long she had been lying there. She hadn't meant to go to sleep. Her mind had been so full of dark thoughts; she had felt so empty. And she still did. A small tear escaped from the corner of her eye to roll into her hairline at the temple.

She was such a waste. She was of no use. Not to herself, not to Linda... not to anyone. If she disappeared from sight this very moment, her body fading into nothingness, would anyone ever know? Would anyone really care? *Yes,* she answered herself dutifully, Linda would. But, as people tended to say, wouldn't her disappearance be a blessing in disguise? It might actually be a relief. Then Linda wouldn't have to have her little sister dragging after her, making so many demands, forcing sacrifices she shouldn't be asked to make.

It wasn't Linda's fault that she had had the accident. She had been thinking about the music playing on the car radio, trying to tune in the station so that the sound would come in better—and it had happened. Her car had veered into the lane of oncoming traffic.

Most times, nothing would have happened. She would have noticed the fault and corrected it. But that time...that one particular time...something did. And a human life had been destroyed. All because of her. Because *she* had wanted to hear a special song.

Melanie turned her face into her pillow as more tears followed the first.

Why hadn't she been the one killed? She'd gladly trade places. She would much rather be dead than have to continue to live with the knowledge of what she'd done. The man was innocent! If only she'd—

No! The plea was silently screamed. She couldn't continue to think about it! Not again...and again! If she did, she'd go mad!

She drew a series of deep breaths, trying to calm herself, trying to tell herself that everything would be all right—just as Linda would say if she were here and knew what she was feeling. Linda, who was always there...and had been for all her life. Melanie didn't know what she would do without her.

The last thought struck an echo in her mind. *She didn't know what she would do without her....*

It was wrong to be so dependent. It hurt her; it hurt Linda. Dependency was like a web, woven with the silk of love, but one that held...and held until the spark that fed that love was eventually destroyed.

Melanie sat up. She didn't know what she would do if she ever lost Linda's love. She wanted to run, to hide, to find a place where pain couldn't follow her.

Then suddenly she became motionless, all thoughts but one erased from her mind. For her entire life she had stood back and let other people guide the way for her. It had been natural; it fitted her personality. But didn't there come a time when it was important that she go her own way? That she take a stand, no matter how small?

Melanie stared at the softly billowing curtains. She had two choices: she could stay dependent and take the chance of losing everything for both Linda and herself, or she could take the first tentative step that would start them on the road to a whole new way of life.

As the curtains continued to dance quietly in the breeze, a small fire was lighted in Melanie's soul...the first flame of self-determination.

LINDA SAT in the back seat of the Jeep, silently castigating herself for her choice of duty. She didn't know what she was doing here with Tate and Patrick, when she should be back at the boardinghouse with Melanie. Her sister was in such a brittle state. What had she been thinking of?

Wind was whipping through the open windows, pulling at her hair, as they drove along the back roads from one claim to another. Miles from town...miles from Melanie. It had been hours since they had started the search, and as the time accumulated, so did her feeling that something was wrong.

When Tate swung around to look at her, she tried to smile, but she wasn't successful in her effort.

A light frown furrowed his brow. "Something wrong?" he asked softly.

Linda shook her head. She didn't want to be the cause of the search being put on hold. Not when she had been the one to invite herself along. She bit the tip of her tongue to keep from speaking.

Tate looked at her steadily. It was easy for him to see that she was troubled. "What is it?" he prompted.

Linda could no longer withhold her concern. "I'm worried about Melanie."

"Why?"

She shook her head. "I don't know. It's just a feeling."

Tate held her gaze for another few seconds before turning to Patrick. "We're going to be taking a break for lunch pretty soon, aren't we?"

Patrick shrugged. "We can."

"Let's take it now."

Patrick glanced from Tate to Linda. He saw the worry reflected in her face and gave an assenting nod.

MORE THAN ONCE as Melanie guided the car along the road that had become familiar to her as a passenger, nightmare remembrances rose up to haunt her, to cripple her, to try and force her back into the quicksand that offered little option. But she held firmly to her determination, knowing that she was doing exactly what she must. She had to do it for Linda. She had to do it for herself.

ROLAND BARNS tried to slip into the boardinghouse unseen. But Bob Tarrant looked up the moment he entered. The proprietor was agitated.

"Where'd you run off to, Roland? I tried to call the office, and no one was there. Then I checked all over town—"

The deputy didn't look in a particularly good frame of mind. "What's up?" he asked.

"It's that girl. That Melanie Conway."

"What about her?"

"She's gone! About a half hour ago. I was upstairs, fixing a sash in a window, and I saw her get into her car and drive away."

The deputy stiffened. "Didn't you try to stop her?"

"Sure I did, but she didn't hear me yell. And by the time I got downstairs, she was gone."

"Where do you think she is?"

"How should I know? But if I had a guess, I'd say that claim of theirs. That sister of hers seems mighty set on working it. Mighty set."

Roland immediately reversed direction.

"Weren't you supposed to be watching her?" Bob Tarrant called after him.

The deputy paused almost imperceptibly as he started out the door. But he didn't turn around. Just as he gave no answer.

MELANIE PUSHED through the underbrush to the gnarled tree, where she paused for a moment to let her eyes run over the claim site. This was the first time she had seen it since the explosion. Her gaze took in the singed grasses, the scattered bits of board. Someone had cleared away the wreckage from beside the stream.

She started down the embankment. She had yet to run the dredge, but she knew that she could do it, if her strength held out. She would *make* it hold out. So much of what had happened was her fault. It was about time that she took some initiative to help bring about a solution.

And if those men came...

She shook her head. The men wouldn't come. They would have to be crazy to show their faces again, if they were the killers.

Melanie knew of the gold Linda and Tate had taken from the stream the day before. If she could get even a quarter of that amount, she would feel that she had contributed.

She crossed the board spanning the stream with ease, then headed toward the lean-to for the hat she had taken to wearing while in the sun.

She was proud of what she was about to do. She would be even prouder when she accomplished her goal.

She opened the door, took a step inside...then found the hard barrel of a gun jammed crudely into her stomach.

As they approached the boardinghouse, Linda's nerves tightened even more. Something was wrong. She knew it!

At her side, Tate was sensitive to her growing unease. He reached out to encircle her shoulders with his arm.

Patrick glanced at them but said nothing.

They were met in the hall by Bob Tarrant. Ethyl was close behind. "We've been wondering what happened!" he exclaimed. "Is she all right?" He looked behind them, as if expecting to see someone else. Then he looked back at them in confusion. "She's not with you?"

Linda's stomach dropped. Her fears were being confirmed.

Patrick's hand had frozen in the act of taking off his hat. "She?" he questioned, already knowing the answer, but hoping that—

"That other Conway girl... Melanie. She left here about an hour ago. I thought you'd know—" he glanced at Linda "—I'm sorry. I didn't mean to—"

Patrick interrupted. "She went off by herself? Where was Roland?"

The landlord shrugged. "That's what I'd like to know. I looked all over town for him. Then I gave up and came back here. He showed up about ten minutes later. Then he went tearing off after her."

Tate was already back at the door. "There's only one place she'd go."

Linda and Patrick quickly followed him.

They didn't get far. After the morning's activities, the Jeep was low on fuel, and they were forced to swerve into the service station.

Typically, the old attendant didn't hurry. His movements were slow, deliberate. Linda wanted to scream. Melanie was out there somewhere, possibly in trouble. If anything happened to her...

The old man capped the tank, then offered to clean the windshield. As Tate tightly declined, the old man leaned closer to the window and stared at the papers resting on the narrow dash. "You lookin' for that man?" he asked.

Tate had already started the engine, impatient to be gone. Who knew what kind of trouble Melanie might be in? He didn't like it that she had been gone so long. Neither was he reassured because Roland had followed her. "Yes," he said, then from reflex asked, "Have you seen him?"

The old man took the papers for a better look. "Might have seen both of 'em. Both kinda big and burly?"

Linda nodded, sitting forward.

"Where'd you see 'em?" Patrick leaned closer from the back seat.

"Saw 'em talkin' to Roland. Wasn't supposed to, but I did. They were behind the old stamp mill."

Ice crystallized in Linda's bloodstream.

"You sure, Jason?" Patrick barked.

The old man nodded. "I'm good at faces."

Linda's eyes were wide with fear as she turned to her companions. "Then that means—"

"It doesn't mean anything," Patrick said shortly, still not wanting to believe the worst of his deputy.

Tate didn't hesitate any longer. "It means we'd better get the hell out of here and find Melanie."

The Jeep raced away from the station, its light bar, seldom used, flashing frantically.

MELANIE TWISTED painfully, trying to sit up. She had been tied, her hands behind her back, and left at the base of one of the trees near the edge of the site. Her bindings were cutting into her wrists and into her chest. Still, she managed to accomplish what she wished.

It took a moment for her to locate the men. She had heard their periodic curses and the clang of materials being moved. Now she could see what they were doing. They were searching through everything, both inside and around the lean-to, throwing pieces this way and that, uncaring of the harm they might do.

She caught her breath. She didn't understand what they were looking for.

One of them paused to glance at her. She quickly averted her gaze. Several moments later she let her eyes slide back. He had gone back to the search.

Melanie strained against the rope. She had to get away!

Moments later her chin dropped in defeat. There was nothing she could do. A section of rope was around the tree's trunk, and short of uprooting it—which she knew she couldn't do—she was fully secured.

Her gaze returned to the men. If they found what they were looking for, what would they do with her? They were the men she and Linda had seen the first day. Were they also the murderers? Murderers... She and Linda... *Linda!* Her mind called the beloved name.

The men suddenly froze. Then, simultaneously, each looked toward the embankment.

Sensing their startled intensity, Melanie looked there, as well.

Bold as brass, Roland Barns was striding across the stream toward them.

Her heart speeded up. If Roland was here, then Patrick and Tate... and Linda!... wouldn't be far behind. Her silent cry for help had been heard!

She struggled once again against her bindings. She felt Roland's gaze sweep over her before moving onto the two men. He calmly started across the crossing board.

Melanie was surprised by his courage. He hadn't seemed that sort previously. Her gaze switched to the two men to see how they were reacting, why they weren't doing anything to stop him.

The men didn't look at all perturbed at being caught out.

"Well, look who's here," the man with the beard jeered. "You forget something, De-pu-ty?"

Roland continued to walk. He motioned toward Melanie. "Why don't you let me take her home? She's not going to give you any trouble."

"Now why should we do that? Because you're asking us *real* nice?"

"I don't want another murder on my conscience, that's why."

The bearded man laughed. "What's one more?"

Roland's hands clenched at his sides. "I didn't *know* anything about the others."

"So you say. Who's going to believe you? Do you believe him, Frank?"

His partner smiled slowly. "Nope. I seem to remember you telling us to do whatever we wanted and you'd cover for us."

Melanie gasped. She could barely believe what she was hearing. Roland was mixed up with the murders? She hadn't liked him, but she would never have credited him with that.

"I didn't mean for you to kill anyone!" Roland denied hotly. "I just wanted you to cause trouble... that's all."

"We like to do things our own way," the clean-shaven man called Frank said mockingly.

His partner's laugh rumbled from deep within him in appreciation of the reply.

"I tried to find you earlier," Roland said angrily. "To tell you to get out."

"You afraid we'll talk if we get caught?"

"There's no reason for *anyone* to get caught! Just leave!"

"And let you have all the gold?"

"What gold?" Roland demanded.

Frank curled his lip. "The fortune in gold that's hidden here, that's what. You're not forgetting about that, are you?"

Roland made an irritated gesture. "There *is* no gold. I only told you that to get you to stay."

"And we're supposed to believe that?" The speaker was incredulous. "You're something, Barns. Really something. You waltz in here, tell us it was all a lie, and we're supposed to leave like meek little choirboys?"

"There *isn't* any hidden gold!"

The bearded man motioned toward Melanie. "She'll tell us."

"She doesn't know anything."

"You want it for yourself."

"I only wanted the job!"

Both men laughed.

Roland lost control. Melanie could see that he had started to tremble. His voice, when he spoke, trembled as well. "Let her go!" he demanded.

Frank turned away slightly, showing his continuing contempt. "Why don't you just leave?" he said.

"Not without her."

Frank slowly turned back. His features were hard, dangerous. "Then you just might not leave yourself."

"You trying to be a he-ro, little man?" the bearded man goaded him.

Roland stared at the two men across from him. Then, without Melanie realizing what he was about to do, he reached for the gun that rested low on his hip. But before he could bring it forward, the clean-shaven outlaw had reached into his shirt and withdrawn the gun he had threatened her with earlier. Only this time when he aimed it, he fired.

The sound was deafening. As Roland's body fell to the ground in a still crumpled heap, Melanie screamed.

Frank ran over to her, drew the gun back... he was about to hit her with it, but held himself in check. "He's not dead—" he grated harshly "—so save your breath. He's not much of one, but I've never killed a lawman in my life, and I don't plan to start now. Riles the others up like killer bees." He paused. "Now, you, on the other hand, I just might kill. If you don't tell me what I what to know."

"I don't know what you're talking about!" Melanie declared, her voice thin and shaky. She had never seen a man shot before.

Frank smiled. "Then I think you might just need a little persuasion." He motioned to his partner. "Let's see if we can get the little lady to remember. Take her to the mine."

Melanie screamed again as the other man came toward her.

INSIDE THE MINE it was dank and cold, and in the half-light Melanie shrank away from the bearded man who had hit her. "You know where it is," he growled. "Tell us!" He raised his hand to strike her once again, but was stopped by his partner.

"Hold it! I have a better idea."

Melanie's breathing was quick and shallow as Frank squatted down beside her. "I think what we'll do is leave you here for awhile. To let you think things over. If you decide to tell us, we'll let you go. If you don't..." His smile was chilling. "If you don't, we're going to bring this place down on top of you." He swept a hand around them. "How do you fancy this for a grave? It's nice and quiet...and it would take that sister of yours years to find you."

Melanie swallowed her fear. "I can't tell you something I don't know! No one told us about any hidden gold. All we were told was that our uncle had started to make a find."

His answer was deceptively patient. "Which means that he found gold. Which means that he might have found a lot of it, and that he hid it someplace!"

Melanie tried to think of an alternative. "If we know about it, why didn't we dig it up ourselves and leave?"

"Because you wanted more."

The man felt his partner grow restive. He stood up. "Now, we're through talking. We're through being nice." He reached for a bracing board and shook it. Numerous tiny rocks cascaded from the ceiling. He laughed as his partner took off for the mine entrance. "Just think about it," he advised softly. "Oh—and we're going to take the lantern. You'll think better in the dark.''

Melanie's heart leaped. "No! Please!"

His smile increased. "Think about it," he said. Then he turned away, the light going with him.

LINDA GAVE an exultant cry when she saw their car parked in the clearing near the claim site. But the sight of the sheriff's second Jeep tempered her joy. Melanie was here, or at least had been, but so was Roland.

As soon as the Jeep she was riding in stopped rolling, Linda jumped out, ready to rush through the brush to the embankment and on to the stream. But Tate hurried to hold her back. "We have to follow Patrick's lead," he urged, even though he understood her desire for haste; he felt it himself.

Patrick moved slowly through the brush and flattened himself at the top of the embankment. With great care, he raised his head to survey the scene. For what seemed to be long moments, he remained still, his body stiff. Then he lowered himself again.

Linda and Tate were stretched out near him. "What is it?" she whispered. "Is she there?" Tate's hand remained on her back.

Patrick's lips were thin. "I didn't see her. But Roland's there. He's down. I didn't see him move."

Panic shot through her. If Roland was there, possibly dead, and Melanie was gone... that could only mean one thing.

Patrick raised his head again, this time even more carefully. When he lowered it, he whispered, "He moved."

Linda's body reacted. She jerked, wanting to take action. "Then let's go ask him where Melanie is! If he's done anything to hurt her—"

Tate tried to calm her. "Running down there isn't going to do any good. What if the men are still here? What if by what we do we make things more difficult for Melanie? We can't chance that."

"But—"

Patrick cut in, his voice filled with authority. "Linda, you stay here. Tate, go off to the right... I'll take the left. Don't show yourself."

Tate's hand moved from Linda's back. Then he, along with Patrick, moved quietly away.

Left alone, Linda rolled onto her back and stared at the great expanse of cloudless sky. Inside her soul she gave the desperate cry she couldn't utter aloud.

What seemed hours later, the men returned. Tate, out of breath, arrived first. "I didn't see anything."

Patrick soon followed. He threw himself down beside them, his chest heaving. When he got back his breath, he said, "I saw both of them. I'm not sure if they saw me or not. They're at the mine."

"What are we going to do?" Linda cried.

Patrick heaved himself to his feet again. "Call for help... then go talk to 'em."

Linda reached for Tate, more to comfort her than to assist her.

THE BEARDED MAN jerked up his head. Like an animal, he had caught a scent. He was in time to see a head disappear behind a large boulder. "Someone's here!" he hissed to his partner, who was leaning against the wall of the cliff just outside the mine entrance. The man was smoking a cigarette and looking at the ground.

Frank threw down the cigarette and hurried inside the mine for cover. His partner followed. Chancing a quick look outside, he leaned forward. "Who was it?" he asked, frowning. "The other deputy?"

"Nah. This guy was older."

"The sheriff?"

"Maybe."

Frank cursed.

The men began to argue. Listening to them, Melanie felt a jolt of optimism for the first time in what seemed ages.

Frank won the argument. He jerked Melanie to her feet and dragged her to just inside the mine entrance. He pulled her close, drew his gun and trained it on her head. "Say something!" he rasped.

Melanie opened her mouth, but nothing came out. He jerked her arm higher behind her. "Say it!" he ordered again.

Melanie tried. "Linda!" she cried.

There was nothing. Then, "I'm here, Melanie!"

Grateful tears sprang into Melanie's eyes.

The man thrust her back into the arms of his friend. He yelled outside, "Let us go, or the girl dies!"

Patrick took a moment to answer. When he did, his voice was calm. "Why don't you just send her out here? Then we can talk."

Frank made a crude reply.

Patrick waited again before saying levelly, "It's only going to get worse the longer you wait. We've put in a call for assistance. If you give up now—let her go unharmed—things will go better for you."

He laughed harshly. "I doubt it."

"You might come out of it alive."

"For how long?" he demanded.

The partner's fingers were grinding into the tender flesh of Melanie's arms. He stank with his fear. "Maybe we should do what he says, Frank."

"Are you crazy?" his partner replied. "They know what we've done."

Melanie spoke up, surprising even herself. "Maybe they don't have proof," she said.

Both men looked at her. If she could keep their attention, take it away from those outside...or even just sow the seeds of doubt...

"My sister and I couldn't help them," she went on. "We didn't even know the bodies were buried here. We—"

"Shut up. Shut up! I have to think!"

"I don't *want* to think," the sweating man who held her said. "I just want to get outta here!"

"Then let me go," she prompted him. "I'll talk to them. I'll tell them that you're not the same men we saw."

"Shut up!" Frank yelled.

The man lifted her from her feet. "I'm going!" he cried hoarsely. "And she's coming with me!"

When he started to run, his partner shouted after him.

Light stabbed into Melanie's eyes as they broke into the afternoon sunshine. The man was using her body as a shield. Only his grip wasn't as good as it could have been, and Melanie used his oversight to twist away, causing him to stumble. They both hit the ground with a hard thud.

LINDA SPRANG to her feet when she saw her sister and the man sprawl on the ground. She didn't care if she was exposed. She had to help Melanie.

Tate grabbed her by the arms and pulled her back down. She read the message in his eyes: he didn't want her to move. With his body held as tightly as a spring, he leaned forward and kissed her hard before jumping from their cover.

Linda immediately returned to where she could see, her gaze fastened on Tate.

Puffs of dust were being kicked up all around his feet. The other man was at the mine opening, his gun drawn and blazing. Tate continued to run.

Linda felt Patrick move beside her. The sun caught a reflection off the metal of his weapon. He steadied it, aimed...and fired. The sound reverberated in her ears.

The man at the mine entrance spun around, hit the cliff wall, then straightened. Blood was oozing from between his fingers as he held onto his left shoulder. Then he, too, started to run, but in the opposite direction.

Patrick descended the knoll like a man half his age. Soon he was splashing along the stream, then into the rocks beyond.

Linda's attention instantly returned to Melanie and Tate. Only a few seconds had passed. Melanie still remained on the ground. But Tate was squaring off with the bearded man, who had assumed a crouch like a sumo wrestler.

For his part, Tate forgot that he was carrying a weapon. It never entered his mind to draw it. Instead, instinctively, he sprang at the man...and felt as if he had hit a brick wall.

Melanie, dazed by her fall, was trying to wriggle out of the way. The two men were fighting almost on top of her. Soon she had assistance. Linda had grabbed her and was pulling her away. In the confusion, the binding at her wrists had come loose and her left arm now hung limp. It might be broken; she didn't know. She could feel nothing.

Fascinated, she watched as Linda then went to Tate's aid. While the bearded man was bent over, hitting him, she jumped on the man's back. Her fingers instantly wound themselves in the dirty mass of his hair and she yanked as hard as she could. The man let out a loud yowl. He tried to get her off.

While his attention was divided, Tate went to work on the man's belly, delivering blow after blow. Finally the man's strength deserted him and he fell to his knees. Linda was pommeling him about the head and shoulders and continued to do so until he was flat on the ground. It took Tate to pull her off.

Patrick soon came up with the clean-shaven man in tow, whose hands were cuffed behind his back. Blood had spread across the front of one side of his shirt and was running down his arm. It was also flowing freely from a fresh cut on his forehead.

Patrick, looking none the worse for wear, threw Tate another set of handcuffs. "Hook him up," he directed.

A moment later the sound of cars arriving and doors being slammed cut through the air.

The cavalry had arrived, but it wasn't needed.

Chapter Sixteen

Linda restlessly thumped the back of the couch before starting to pace once again. Last night Tate had told her he would see her as soon as he could the next morning. It was now morning. It was time for him to arrive.

As she paced, she limped slightly. She had no idea when she had hurt her ankle. She had no memory of pain. Not until she had gotten out of bed for a drink of water and winced as she put her foot to the floor. But then so much had happened at the claim. Time had seemed frozen, yet it had sped by.

When she closed her eyes, even now she could see Melanie held against the man as he ran, looking so much like a rag doll in the arms of an uncaring giant. She could see Tate, being shot at as he ran. She could see herself, mounted on the giant's back, trying to make him stop hurting Tate. She had given in to anger then and to her pent-up fear. She hadn't really thought, just acted.

Linda released a tense sigh. After reinforcements had arrived, Tate had held her and whispered that it was over. But it didn't seem over. Her mind might tell her that it was, yet doubts remained.

Her eyes fell on the gun resting on a period writing desk. She had brought it down with her that morning to return to Bob Tarrant. It was the one he had given her that day at the claim... which seemed a thousand years ago, not just two days. She didn't want to see it again; she didn't want to have need of it any longer. Yet without it were she and Melanie safe?

Linda gave a soft groan. Of course they were safe. The two men who had been terrorizing them were in custody in Sacramento, and from what Melanie had told the police, they were the same men who had killed the prospectors. Everything could now settle back to normal.

But what *was* normal?

Linda's clothes were packed and waiting in her room. She would pack Melanie's as soon as she awakened. She was sure Melanie wouldn't feel up to doing it on her own, not with her arm in a cast.

Perhaps they should wait another day or two before returning to the claim. Perhaps she was pushing too hard, too soon.

Linda turned toward the door, her heartbeat quickening. She thought she'd heard someone approach.

PATRICK SEEMED in no hurry. His movements, as he stirred sugar into his cup, were slow and deliberate. His expression was weighted heavily with sadness.

Tate pulled his own cup closer, took a sip, then pushed it away. He was anxious to see Linda, to talk with her, to reassure himself that all was well. Turning off worry wasn't like shutting off a spigot. There were no absolutes. But he couldn't leave Patrick in such a mood. He couldn't desert him.

He cleared his throat, looking for something to say. "I'm glad Roland wasn't seriously hurt."

Patrick nodded.

"I don't think he knew what he was getting into, Patrick. It all seems to have gotten away from him."

His old friend looked up. "You're defending him?"

"He did try to help Melanie."

"Which makes everything all right?"

"I didn't say that."

"*Nothing* makes what he did right!"

"No." Tate studied his friend's face. The hard edge from the day before was still present; Patrick would never again doubt his abilities. But he had been deeply hurt by Roland's betrayal. Patrick did nothing halfway. If he decided to help someone, he would move heaven and earth to help him. And he expected nothing in return...except basic loyalty, something Roland seemed to be deficient in. Still, Patrick would mourn his loss—a waste of time as far as Tate was concerned. "He's not worth it, Patrick," he said softly, trying to get his friend to see reason.

Patrick leveled a look at him. "Some used to say the same about you."

Tate took the reprimand cleanly. He was sure what Patrick said was true. "Had he been in trouble before?" he asked curiously.

Patrick nodded.

"He isn't from around here, is he?"

"No. He's from Nevada. Reno. His mother... his mother was a friend of mine."

Tate said nothing.

Patrick rubbed his face. He was sore in places he hadn't ached in for years. But the tenderness of his body was nothing compared to the soreness of his soul. He looked across at Tate, saw the child, then the man. What he had to say was difficult for him. "It's possible— It's possible that Roland is my son."

Tate stared at him. If he had been hit by a bolt of lightning, he couldn't have been more dumbfounded. "You're... not sure?"

Patrick shook his head. Pain made his voice gruff as he admitted, "I didn't even know he was alive until a year ago. His mother and I—"

"You don't have to explain," Tate interrupted. He would never betray his friend's confidences, but he didn't want him to say anything that he might later regret.

"But I do!" Patrick contradicted. "I get lonely sometimes, Tate. Not so much now. But when I was younger..."

Tate wasn't interested in judging Patrick. Few men could lay claim to such an exalted position. Especially not him. He searched for something to say. "He did try to help Melanie. That took a lot of courage." When Patrick made no reply, he asked, "Do you think he'll come back here after everything gets sorted out?"

"I doubt it."

"Do you want him to?"

"I'm not sure."

"Would you like me to talk with him?"

Patrick shook his head. "If anyone talks with him, it has to be me. I saw him last night when I took his statement, but he didn't feel much like talking then... at least, that's what he said."

"He probably didn't." Tate defended the younger deputy for Patrick's sake.

Patrick made no comment. He pushed away from the table. "Well, I'm off." A sudden glint struggled against the sadness in his eyes. "You be sure to tell the girls I send my compliments. And tell them I'll stop by later. Not for anything official—that can wait. I just thought I'd..." He didn't finish.

Tate took direction from Patrick's attempt to lighten their conversation. "I'll tell them," he said.

"I'm sure you will," Patrick murmured, and a glimmer of a smile tweaked his beard.

Tate followed his friend from the house. They stood side by side on the porch, one unconsciously mirroring the position of the other. Then, in accord, each went his separate way.

MELANIE YAWNED lightly as she entered the parlor. Her left arm was sore and heavy in its cast, one cheek was bruised and swollen. Yesterday still had a surreal air. Almost as if it hadn't happened, in direct contradiction to all the evidence.

She smiled at Linda, who had looked up at her expectantly.

Linda tried to mask her disappointment. "Good morning," she called. Then before she could stop it, "You look awful."

Melanie's lopsided smile increased. "I've looked in the mirror."

"Does your arm still hurt?"

Melanie touched the cast protectively. "A little." When Linda moved, Melanie saw her limp slightly. "Did you get hurt, too? I wouldn't be surprised. You should have seen yourself."

"No, thank you. I'd rather not."

"You were on that man's back like a burr."

"Melanie!"

Melanie came to hug her. "I thought you were wonderful."

"I'd just as soon forget it ever happened. I don't ever want to go through a day like that again."

Melanie considered the statement to see whether she agreed. Somehow she felt stronger for what had occurred. It was as if she had taken a test and won top honors, or at least placed high. She hadn't folded when the men treated her roughly. She had continued to resist, even when things had looked blackest. In her own small way, she had exhibited some of the Conway grit. Maybe she was a Conway to be proud of, after all. At least it was something to think about. "It wasn't so bad," she said.

Linda drew back to look at her. She saw the new spark of determination in her sister's eyes. Melanie was still physically weak, that was readily apparent, but a change had come over her spirit. Linda said softly, "No, maybe it wasn't."

At that moment Tate entered the room. He paused, wondering if he was interrupting something he shouldn't. Then both sisters looked at him and smiled.

Tate nodded at each, but was drawn to Linda. His arm slipped around her waist, as if he had performed the action a million times. She felt so good to touch. He gave her a special smile before scrutinizing Melanie. "How would you feel if you ended up with a black eye?" he asked her.

Melanie blinked. "You think I might?"

"It's possible."

Melanie grinned proudly. "I've never had one before."

Tate turned back to Linda. "You're all right?" he asked softly.

Now she was, Linda thought. "I'm fine."

A moment was lost for each of them. Melanie watched, loath to break their intimacy.

Tate pulled back first. If he didn't, the town would have some new gossip to add to the old.

Linda, blushing lightly, needlessly straightened her hair.

"How's Patrick?" Melanie asked, helping to bridge the gap of silence.

Tate said, "I think he's going to be all right. Now that the cause of his trouble is gone."

"You think people will be back on his side?"

"No doubt about it."

"What about Roland?" Linda asked.

"Last I heard his condition was upgraded. He should be out of the hospital in a day or two."

"What will happen to him then?" Melanie asked.

Tate shrugged.

"I'd like to thank him," she said shyly.

"For what?" Linda asked, shocked.

"For trying to help me."

Linda didn't make another protest. It would be a waste of time and effort. Melanie was Melanie.

"I wonder what Mrs. Armbruster will have to say?" Melanie went on to muse. "I mean... I feel sorry for her. Linda and I know what it's like to lose a father. But she acted so hateful. I hope she apologizes to Patrick."

"I wouldn't hold my breath," Tate murmured.

Melanie giggled softly. "No, she's not the sort, is she?"

Tate's hand smoothed across Linda's ribs. She shivered at his touch.

Melanie saw the exchange. She said, "I think I'm going to see what Mrs. Tarrant has made for breakfast. Shall I tell her you'll be coming along a little later?"

Linda nodded.

Melanie started for the door, but detoured to Tate instead. She smiled up at him, glanced at Linda, gave a wicked grin, then reached up to kiss him. "If things had been different," she said softly, "I could have fallen in love with you myself." Then, still smiling, she left the room.

Linda moved restively, uncomfortably aware that Melanie had put into words something that was yet to be stated. "Maybe I'd better go with her," she said as an excuse. "She might need help."

Tate blocked her way. "No, she doesn't."

"But, Tate—"

"Melanie used to need you, but she doesn't anymore. At least, not in the same way. Give her some space, Linda. Give her some time. I think you'll be pleased by what turns up."

"But—"

"Don't be embarrassed."

"I'm not!"

"You are. And you don't have any reason to be. Give me your hand."

"What?" Suddenly everything was going too fast for her. She felt dazed, confused.

"Give me your hand," he repeated.

Linda slowly obeyed.

Tate brought her palm up to his chest, where he gently spread her fingers against his warmth. His voice was edged with huskiness as he said, "I know we haven't had a lot of time. So many things have been happening, but— Do you feel that?"

Linda's eyes were huge as she looked up at him. His heart was beating strongly beneath her hand. It was vibrant, alive. She felt herself begin to tremble.

"It's yours," he said simply.

Linda caught her breath. So many things *had* happened. She wasn't sure she was still the same person she used to be. She used to be so sure of what had to be done—of her part in everything. Now she was sure of little. Except for two things: her abiding love for her sister, and her newly found love for this man.

"I love you, Linda," Tate said softly. "I want you to be my wife."

Linda didn't know what to say. Unlike some women, she had never rehearsed this moment. It had always seemed so faraway. "I never—" She started, stopped, then started again. "I never thought..."

Tate smiled. "Do I take that as a yes?"

Linda nodded solemnly.

Just as solemnly, he reached out to cup the underside of her chin and lift it. Then he lowered his head until his lips could touch hers, gently at first, then with a growing fire that made additional words unnecessary. At that moment Tate loved her more than he had thought possible.

Epilogue

Melanie slipped into the bedroom where Linda had gone to change after the ceremony. She smiled tenderly as she helped her usually competent older sister with the buttons her fingers seemed unable to negotiate.

"It was beautiful, Linda," she said softly. "*You* looked beautiful. And Tate... I don't think I've ever seen a man more proud."

Linda was spilling over with emotion. She was happy, excited.... Her smile was sparkling. "Sometimes I still don't believe it. It doesn't seem real."

Melanie grinned. "Check out that ring you're wearing. I think it's positively decadent that Tate found the gold himself, then had it made into a ring."

Linda touched the delicate gold band. Tate had asked a friend to make the ring, and it was etched with a circling pattern of interlocking hearts. "It's beautiful, too, isn't it?" she said softly.

Melanie hugged her. "Everything is beautiful at a moment like this."

Linda clung to her sister. They had been through so much together. So much, that they could never be truly apart. One would always be a permanent part of the other. Moisture came into her eyes and she had to sniff. Her emotions were so close to the surface. It was as easy to cry as to laugh. But the tears would not be from unhappiness.

Melanie pulled away. Tears were in her eyes, too, and her smile was now wobbly. "I'm going to miss you," she said.

"I will you, too."

"No, you won't."

"I will!"

Melanie relented. "Well, maybe just a little."

Linda smiled. "You'll be all right tomorrow?"

"Of course."

Three months ago there would have been no question of an "Of course." Three months ago they had come to California because they had no money to save the ranch...and three months ago Melanie hadn't been strong enough to take on the task of settling their debts alone, which was something she wanted to do now. To prove to herself that she could.

"Of course," Linda repeated. She looked about the room. She had hung her special dress in the closet where Patrick said she could leave it until she was ready to pick it up. Nothing else was strewn about. Her gaze came back to Melanie. "I guess it's time to go," she said softly.

Melanie nodded.

Linda reached out to hug her again. "Be happy, sweetheart," she whispered.

Melanie patted her hair. "Isn't that what I'm supposed to say to you?"

"We'll say it to each other," Linda decided.

The sisters broke apart and kissed the other's cheeks. Then they went downstairs to the waiting people.

TATE LAUGHED as he shook bits of rice from his hair. Linda was brushing herself off, as well, when he took the moment to kiss her, long and almost satisfactorily. "Are you happy?" he asked.

"Deliriously," she replied.

That seemed to be the answer he wanted to hear. The car's engine sprang to life and they drew away from the tiny group of people waving to them from Patrick's front porch.

A few minutes later, Linda asked, "Are you?"

Tate didn't need further explanation of her question. He was starting to know her so well now; he was beginning to know how she thought. "Definitely," he said.

She probed deeper. "About everything?"

"About everything."

She leaned close, placing her cheek against his shoulder. "I still think you only married me for my money."

He took his eyes from the road long enough to kiss the tip of her nose. "Of course," he teased. "What else? I certainly don't love you."

"I think you do," she contradicted him.

"I think you're right."

Linda hugged his arm. She felt so right beside him. So...complete. It was as if she had always known him.

She sighed, thinking of the days ahead, the days at the small hotel at Lake Tahoe where they would have only each other to think about, to enjoy, to continue making discoveries with. Then she thought of Melanie and what her sister was about to do. She needed reassurance. "Do you think everything will go all right for Melanie tomorrow?"

"The lawyer said it would."

Linda was quiet for a moment. "And you're sure you don't mind taking all that time off next year to help get the ranch back into operation?"

"I wouldn't have offered if I had."

"You might have second thoughts, once you get into it. It's hard work."

"Are you planning to sit on your backside and watch?"

Linda grinned. She loved the way he teased her. "No."

"Living on campus isn't going to be a holiday, either. You might come to regret agreeing to do that, too."

For a fleeting moment he thought of Miriam. He had written to her, explaining. In return, he had received a postcard from Cyprus. "Having a wonderful time. Glad for you that you're not here!" And her signature. As he had suspected, she held no regrets, just as he wouldn't if the tables had been turned.

He trailed his hand along Linda's thigh, enjoying the sensation.

In the rearview mirror, he saw the last vestiges of Amador Springs recede from view. A letter had brought him here—a letter that at the time he wished he had not received. If only he had known.

Linda noted the turnoff to the claim. She and Melanie had come seeking gold and they had found it. But they had also learned that not everything that gleamed golden was a precious metal. Some things were *much* more precious. Some people.

She shifted so that she could watch her husband. After a moment he glanced at her and warned, "We may not make it to Tahoe if you keep looking at me that way."

"Is that a threat?" she challenged.

Tate found a turnout that was protected from the road by a growth of trees. He cut the engine and faced her. "You just can't resist taunting me, can you?"

"Do you really want me to stop?"

"No."

Linda traced her fingers through the dark hair over his ear. "Well, then—" she murmured and smiling softly, leaned close to nibble the tender flesh.

Tate didn't need a second invitation.

Harlequin Regency Romance™

Romance the way it was *always* meant to be!

The time is 1811, when a Regent Prince rules the empire. The place is London, the glittering capital where rakish dukes and dazzling debutantes scheme and flirt in a dangerously exciting game. Where marriage is the passport to wealth and power, yet every girl hopes secretly for love....

Welcome to Harlequin Regency Romance where reading is an adventure and romance is *not* just a thing of the past! Two delightful books a month, beginning May '89.

Available wherever Harlequin Books are sold.

REG-1

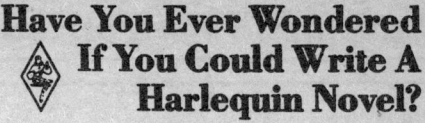

Have You Ever Wondered If You Could Write A Harlequin Novel?

Here's great news—Harlequin is offering a series of cassette tapes to help you do just that. Written by Harlequin editors, these tapes give practical advice on how to make your characters—and your story—come alive. There's a tape for each contemporary romance series Harlequin publishes.

Mail order only

All sales final

TO: *Harlequin Reader Service*
Audiocassette Tape Offer
P.O. Box 1396
Buffalo, NY 14269-1396

I enclose a check/money order payable to HARLEQUIN READER SERVICE® for $9.70 ($8.95 plus 75¢ postage and handling) for EACH tape ordered for the total sum of $_____*
Please send:

- ☐ Romance and Presents
- ☐ American Romance
- ☐ Superromance
- ☐ Intrigue
- ☐ Temptation
- ☐ All five tapes ($38.80 total)

Signature_____
(please print clearly)
Name:_____
Address:_____
State:_____ Zip:_____

*Iowa and New York residents add appropriate sales tax.

AUDIO-H

Harlequin American Romance®

COMING NEXT MONTH

#289 FULL HOUSE by Jackie Weger

Justine's house was full... of complications. She had plenty to do just adjusting to life after divorce, making a new home for her kids, and struggling to keep her mother and ex-mother-in-law from tearing what security she'd managed to build to bits. But Tucker, her handsome neighbor, was a complication she found hard to resist—especially when she found out about the dilapidated old house's other occupant: Lottie Roberts, a 159-year-old ghost.

#290 HOME TO THE COWBOY by Bobby Hutchinson

The new vet in Bitterroot, Montana, Sara Wingate, was up to her ears in muck and squealing pigs when she first met rancher Mitch Carter. A former rodeo hero, Mitch had reluctantly returned to work the family spread. How long would it be before wanderlust hit him again? Or had Mitch come home for good?

#291 TOGETHER ALWAYS by Dallas Schulze

The moment he'd set eyes on the pale, pretty child, Trace Dushane knew why he lived. Over the years he'd kept Lily from harm, fed her, sheltered her. Now he had to convince her she no longer needed him. That was the hardest part of all—for the first time facing a life without Lily.

#292 ROBBING THE CRADLE by Anne Henry

Lots of women dated younger men, but could thirty-year-old Dallas caterer and mother of two small boys, Pam Sullivan, do it? Persistent Joel Bynum was "that nice young man at the supermarket." He was a college kid, for heaven's sake! Could Pam throw caution to the winds?

COMING IN MARCH FROM
Harlequin Superromance

Book Two of the Merriman County Trilogy
AFTER ALL THESE YEARS
the sizzle of Eve Gladstone's
One Hot Summer continues!

Sarah Crewes is at it again, throwing Merriman County into a tailspin with her archival diggings. In *One Hot Summer* (September 1988) she discovered that the town of Ramsey Falls was celebrating its tricentennial one year too early.

Now she's found that Riveredge, the Creweses' ancestral home and property, does not rightfully belong to her family. Worse, the legitimate heir to Riveredge may be none other than the disquieting Australian, Tyler Lassiter.

Sarah's not sure why Tyler's in town, but she suspects he is out to right some old wrongs—and some new ones!

The unforgettable characters of *One Hot Summer* and *After All These Years* will continue to delight you in book three of the trilogy. Watch for *Wouldn't It Be Lovely* in November 1989.

SR349-1

Harlequin Intrigue.

They went in through the terrace door. The house was dark, most of the servants were down at the circus, and only Nelbert's hired security guards were in sight. It was child's play for Blackheart to move past them, the work of two seconds to go through the solid lock on the terrace door. And then they were creeping through the darkened house, up the long curving stairs, Ferris fully as noiseless as the more experienced Blackheart.

They stopped on the second floor landing. "What if they have guns?" Ferris mouthed silently.

Blackheart shrugged. "Then duck."

"How reassuring," she responded. Footsteps directly above them signaled that the thieves were on the move, and so should they be.

For more romance, suspense and adventure, read Harlequin Intrigue. Two exciting titles each month, available wherever Harlequin Books are sold.

INTA-1